For those in need of a little redemption

CHAPTER 1

IT WAS THE devil's hour on Aventum Angelorum, Goetia's own high holy day, and there was a black wind blowing off Tabor's mine. It slithered down the mountain past the places where the old gods of the continent had once held sway. It rolled through the mining town below, called Goetia, snatching hats off heads and shivering shoulders. It wormed its way through the holiday merrymakers on Perdition Street, whispering memories of heavenly war, of bright Lucifer's doomed defiance, and the sweet aftertaste of rebellion cloyed noses and mouths, making those who breathed it in discontent and covetous.

When it hit the Eden, Perdition Street's premiere gambling and drinking establishment, it nearly blew the place down. Wood hit sharp against wood as the front doors flew open, and the glass pane bearing the saloon's moniker cracked straight through. The ruckus drew startled screams and cries of drunken surprise from the patrons, masked faces turning to see what, or who, had entered. A few of the witchier clientele threw a hex to turn evil away, but there was enough vice already squatting in the Eden that whatever extra ungodliness the wind blew in didn't faze most of the regulars.

At first, Celeste Semyaza didn't even feel that old wind licking against her cheek. She was sitting in the dealer's chair at the faro table, focused on the game before her. But when the cards jumped up, kings and jack fools dancing wild in the sudden gale, she spread her hands across the cards to keep 'em down. The three players in front of her did the same, stretching arms and bodies over potential winners... and inevitable losers.

Hypatia, the owner of the Eden, six feet tall and built solid as one of those cursed-up mountains that encircled the town, rushed forward to secure the doors. She paused long enough to let a costumed couple slip through, the woman clutching the tip of a papier-mâché wing as the man, unsteady on high-heeled boots shaped like goat's feet, leaned into her. They stumbled to the bar, where Zeke, the resident bartender, awaited them. But Celeste didn't even notice them, already focused back on the card game.

"Place your bets," she told the players now that the wind had quieted down.

An Elect man sporting a bowler hat and an impressive yellow mustache held his bet, gesturing for the other players to go first. Celeste eyed him, suspicious. He wasn't one of her regulars, so she figured he must be in town for the holiday. Nothing unusual there, but he was worth keeping an eye on.

The man to Mustache's right bore the Mark of the Fallen, that telltale ring of gold around dark eyes and a pair of curling ram's horns. The Fallen man took the opportunity to lay down ten chips on the three of spades.

A mysterious woman in a wide-brimmed blue hat and matching veil extended a long-nailed hand to carefully set a dozen chips on the queen.

The revelry of the Eden had picked back up. The ill wind that had forced its way past the doors of paradise was quickly forgotten to the pleasure of gin slings and gambling. Somewhere nearby, a saloon girl laughed loudly.

The mustachioed man still hadn't laid his bet, and Celeste tapped her fingertips against the felt loudly.

"Where's that singer I heard about?" he asked with lazy indifference. His gaze flickered to the stage next to the piano on the far side of the room as his fingers tripped across a steadily shrinking stack of chips. "Heard she's a beauty with an impressive set of—"

"That's my sister." Celeste cut him off.

"—lungs." He glanced at the dealer, whistling low. "Well, I'll be. Mariel Semyaza's your sister? But you don't have the..." He touched a finger to his eye.

He wasn't the first to notice she didn't have the Mark and wouldn't be the last. "I favor our daddy."

His face scrunched up, puckered sour as a lemon. "A half-breed, then? Well, well."

Celeste kept a small dagger up her sleeve in a sheath attached to her forearm. It was an ingenious thing that Zeke had made for her, meant to shoot the blade down into her hand, hilt to palm, with just a twist of the wrist.

"Watch your tongue, Mister," she said, low and matter-of-fact, "assuming you want to keep it."

He had a dry, unpleasant kind of laugh, more wild dog than man. "Now, don't get your back up."

"Then don't talk about my sister."

"I'm only being friendly."

"I don't need friends. What I need you to do is place your bet."

He sucked at his teeth, fingers still idling over chips.

Finally, the woman in blue spoke, her voice a soft, sibilant hiss. "Place your bet or make room for someone who will.

You're holding up the game."

The Fallen man grumbled in agreement, so with a put-upon sigh, Mustache dropped half a dozen chips on the eight card.

Satisfied, Celeste drew the soda card and placed it to the side. Next, she drew the loser—an eight. Mustache groaned. He'd lost the round.

"Not your night, is it?" the Fallen man next to him observed lightly.

Celeste drew the winner, and the veiled player yawped a muted cry of joy before raking her winnings close. Celeste gave her a congratulatory nod and had begun to reset for the next round when she felt it. She thought for a moment maybe that wind had come on back, but the cards were as still as a spooked-up church mouse. Yet there was *something* at the back of her neck. A breath, a touch. She couldn't describe it except to say it was a wrongness.

She glanced behind her, but there was only the wall. She told herself it was just the ten-cent man at her table getting under her skin, but even as she thought it, she knew it was a lie.

"We playin'?" the man in question asked, voice turned mean with losing.

She almost said yes, but her eyes cut to the empty stage, and the word stuck in her craw. Where was Mariel? Maybe that was the bad feeling that had caught hold of her neck. Mariel should have been up there singing, keeping the crowd cooled.

Celeste waved, trying to get Hypatia's attention, but the woman was holding court at the corner of the bar, telling one of her infamous tall tales, and couldn't spare a glance her way.

She scratched at her neck, unable to shake that bad notion, like someone was throwing a hell of a hex, and promptly said, "Table's closed."

A groan circled the table.

"The game's not done!" Mustache's outrage turned up a notch.

"It's done when I say it's done," Celeste said. "There are other tables. Find yourself another if you don't like it."

"But I've got money invested in this one." His voice was practically a shout, and people paused over their drinks or in the middle of their stories, noticing. His hand strayed down toward his belt, and Celeste saw the butt of a revolver there. She calculated the odds of the man drawing down on her on account of feeling cheated and decided she didn't like them.

Her eyes flickered back to Hypatia. This time, the woman was watching.

"That's money the house won fair and square," Celeste said carefully.

"And I need a chance to win it back. I've got to get a ticket on that new airship to the capital, and this here's only half of what I need."

"Not sure that's on the dealer," the Fallen man said, eyes cutting in sympathy toward Celeste. "You've had poor luck all night, friend."

"And your luck's about to be worse if you don't stay out of this, *friend*," he retorted, hand still hovering over his revolver.

Calm everybody down, Celeste thought. *That's what Hypatia would say. And also, don't kill the customers, especially when they're lining your coffers.*

She lifted her hands. "All right, then, Mister. One more round. Give you a chance to win your money back, and then we're even."

Mustache grinned and let his hand drift back up toward his card. "Now, that's more civilized." He motioned for Zeke to send over a fresh drink. "And maybe we can get that sister of yours to come on out and show us her lungs."

The dagger was in her hand before he'd sucked in a breath to laugh—and through his hand before he'd made a sound.

"I said don't talk about my sister!"

He froze, staring, before he started screaming. Hollering like she'd stuck him in the heart instead of just the hand. He reared back, trying to get free, and his loose arm swept wide, sending drinks and chips flying.

The room dissolved into chaos. Someone was shouting murder, maybe one of Mustache's companions, and then someone else was throwing a punch, and the blue-veiled woman's hat tumbled off, revealing alligator scales and a forked tongue.

Celeste scooped the house winnings into a sack, dragged the dealing box in with them, and dropped low to the ground, just in time to miss a bullet flying past to lodge into the wall behind her. She glanced up and spied Hypatia grabbing the shooter by the neck, disarming him with a vicious chop, and dragging him bodily toward the front door. Celeste shifted directions, crawling out the other side. A crowd had gathered to watch the fight, some of the drunker patrons joining in. She kept her head low and worked her way through the rough-and-tumble, dodging the worst of it.

"Zeke!" she shouted over the din once she'd reached the bar. Zeke had a shotgun in hand and was busy guarding the spirits lining the back wall, making people think twice about taking advantage of the ruckus to try to steal what wasn't theirs. "Have you seen Mariel?"

He grinned, eyes bright, his boyishly handsome face flushed. He was clearly enjoying himself. "Said she wasn't feeling well," he yelled back. "She's lying down in the back for a while. Want me to rouse her?"

She looked across the room to where the back offices were.

There were at least ten men between her and that door, all looking like they'd love to join in the row. "No. If she can sleep through this, then let her. I'll have a smoke and wait it out."

"Want me to send Hypatia out?"

She glanced over her shoulder. A few other punters had joined in the fight, and Hypatia was in the middle of it all, banging heads together, looking happy as a pig in shit.

"Wouldn't want to interrupt."

Zeke grinned and sent her off with a salute.

Celeste slipped out into the back alley, avoiding the mess she'd made.

CHAPTER 2

IT WAS BLESSEDLY empty out back behind the Eden, if not particularly quiet. Somewhere someone was singing loud and drunk enough to wake the dead, and piano music echoed down the dirt road through open saloon doors. Laughter spilled from intoxicated lips, and the faintest scent of opium tinged the night air. Normally, three a.m. found Goetia aslumber, but Aventum Angelorum only happened once a year, and people made the most of it. Even at this hour, Perdition Street bustled.

The holiday was the commemoration of the end of Lucifer's rebellion and the war that followed, although whether one marked it as a celebration or a day of mourning depended entirely on which side of the war one's ancestors had been on. The citizens of Goetia were mostly Elect, so the morning had seen a parade down Main Street and speeches by the local politicians. In the afternoon, those same upstanding denizens poured into the exhibition hall to ooh and aah over the latest mining innovations and wondrous clockwork creations powered by the divinity that came out of those mines. There had even been a charity dinner at the mayor's mansion, with society ladies in taffeta and silk.

But by nightfall, even the most God-fearing of Goetia set aside their righteousness and joined the Fallen down on Perdition. Everywhere there were men and women, Elect and Fallen, rich and poor, dressed as devils, angels, and any manner of hellish creature roaming the streets. Horns and wings were the order of the day, but there were the occasional satyr's cloven foot and a blackened halo made of painted straw.

That's not to say the Elect and the Fallen were at odds in Goetia the other days of the year. They needed each other, in a wretched sort of way. The Fallen were the only ones who could spot the divinity lode for mining, a gift of their ancestry. The Elect paid fair wages for that service and for the other talents of the Fallen that kept Goetia booming. But amid the iniquity of Perdition was the only place they mixed as equals. Everywhere else, Elect were on top and Fallen somewhere below.

Celeste was halfway done with her cigarillo when out came Hypatia, her curls in disarray and a wide smile on her generous mouth. She swiped blood from the corner of her lips, leaving a crimson trail across one cheek.

"How goes it?" Celeste asked, eyes askance on the blood.

Hypatia laughed. "Invigorating!"

Hypatia claimed she was the descendant of the eponymous Alexandrian philosopher and mathematician, but everyone knew her name was Mary and that she hailed from the middle of the continent. Times like these, when her guard was down, Celeste could hear the prairie in her voice.

"And the man?"

She turned a baleful eye to Celeste. "You mean the one you stabbed?"

"That's the one," she said, flat as pan water.

"What did I tell you about that, Celeste?"

"Not to do it, but you didn't hear him, Hyp. He was disrespecting Mariel."

"Mariel's a grown woman and can defend herself. She doesn't need you stepping in to maim a man for every little slight."

"She wasn't there to defend herself, so I did it." Celeste paused. "Maim? So he'll live?"

Hypatia sighed gustily. "He'll live, but you better hope he doesn't bring the law down on us." She leaned over, palm open to Celeste. In her hand was Celeste's dagger. "You've got to think before you do these things."

Celeste took the blade and fitted it back into her trick holster. "And if I said I was sorry?"

"It'd be a start, assuming you meant it."

Celeste was quiet. Hypatia grunted. "That's what I thought."

Something crashed loudly inside, and Hypatia muttered about expensive furniture and glass that was hard to replace, but she said, "Ah, hell, Zeke can handle it. I'm getting too old for this shit." She withdrew a flask, unscrewed it, and drank deeply.

Celeste watched her, amused. "I'll never understand why you own a bar but insist on carrying your own."

"That shit in there is watered to piss," Hypatia admitted, coughing lightly. "This is the good stuff, straight from the barrel. You want?"

"Better not. I've got to get Mariel home later."

Hypatia rolled her shoulders. "Don't be such a biddy, Celeste. I swear, that half-Elect blood of yours keeps you wound tighter than a rich man's asshole."

Celeste bristled. She wanted to protest that watching out for her baby sister had nothing to do with her being mixed-blood, but she was worried there was some truth in Hypatia's observation, although not the way she meant it. Celeste could pass as Elect, but Mariel could not, and that left Celeste with a certain obligation to look out for her sister, especially on a night when free license moved the hearts of men in wicked ways. But she didn't feel like explaining it all to Hypatia, especially when she wasn't sure she had the words for it, anyhow.

"Maybe so," she conceded, tossing her spent cigarillo to the ground before crushing it with her heel. "Think I'll go wake her up anyhow and get home."

"You sure? There's still plenty of merrymaking to be had." She gestured at the night. "Costumed revelry. It's not too late join in." The older woman looked her up and down. "How old are you? Twenty-two?"

"Twenty-three."

"Almost a spinster. It's about time you stopped slumming it down here with us, anyhow. Find yourself some Elect gentleman who'll marry you and make you respectable." Her tone was light, but Celeste could tell she meant it. "I'll never understand why you spend your time down here when you could be up there, living the life."

"You know why." Celeste's voice was hard. "Besides, you're well past thirty, and I don't see you on the arm of a man."

"And you never will." Hypatia pulled from her flask again. "It's different for us full-bloods, and you know it."

And that stung more than Celeste liked. "Good night, Hypatia."

"Wait, I was going to ask you, what do you think of that new saloon girl?"

"Which one?" she asked, a touch exasperated. "You go through a half dozen girls a month."

"The short one with the fringe and the dimples."

"She seems nice," she said diffidently. She couldn't, in fact, place a face with Hypatia's description.

"Nice in the sack, too." Hypatia waggled her thick eyebrows, enough to make Celeste laugh.

"I'm not shacking up with a saloon girl, either."

"Her name's Lilitha, and why not? Haven't you ever wanted someone, Celeste?"

"You know I have," she said, working hard to keep the bitterness out of her voice, "but it didn't work out."

"Aw, hell." Hypatia had the grace to look embarrassed. "Abraxas. Look, I didn't mean to bring him up, I just—"

"Forget it. That's long over, and nothing's changing that. Now all I want is to go home and get some sleep."

"I wish you'd tell me what happened."

"There's nothing to tell," she lied. "It's just… complicated. Besides, it doesn't matter now. I've got everything I need."

"You mean Mariel?"

"And faro. Assuming I'm not out of a job after tonight."

Hypatia allowed her to change the subject. "Naw, that was just the kind of excitement that keeps the Eden top pick on Perdition Street. Don't want us getting a reputation for respectability, do we?"

Celeste smiled, grateful for the grace. "Heaven forfend."

"I'm just saying that if you don't let anybody in… well, it's a lonely life you set yourself up for. Mariel won't stick around for long. She'll marry soon enough, and nobody's life ambition is to deal faro."

"Let it go, Hypatia," Celeste growled, and then her brain stuttered over Hypatia's last words. "Wait, what do you mean Mariel's marrying?"

The door between them banged open, and Celeste jumped, nervous as a jackrabbit.

"Celeste!" It was Zeke, and he was panting like he'd run a mile instead of thirty feet. "You've got to come quick!"

"More trouble?" Hypatia asked.

"It's Mariel, isn't it?" Celeste asked. This was the trouble that had been breathing down her neck, now come home to roost. She looked at Zeke, hoping to hell she was wrong, but his face said she'd told true.

"Sheriff's here, and he's got Virtues with him. They're dragging her out right now."

Virtues were the highest of the Elect. They might only be human, but they were sworn in service to the Orders of the Archangels.

"What the hell for?" asked Hypatia.

"I would've come as soon as they got here, but I was settling things after the tussle like you told me to, and I didn't register them until it was too late."

"Which Order is it?" Celeste asked.

None of the Orders were fond of the Fallen, but at least some of them were benevolent. The Order of Raphael were healers, and the Order of Chamuel were justice keepers and peacemakers. Maybe it wasn't as bad as it felt.

"The Order of Michael." Zeke looked sorry when he said it.

Celeste flinched. The Order of Michael were soldiers, and their loathing for the Fallen was well documented. If they'd come for Mariel, then nothing good would follow.

"How many?" she asked.

"Word is a dozen, at least, and there's an Azrael among 'em."

"Aw, hell," Hypatia muttered.

The Order of Azrael were murderers, no two ways to say it. They might claim their executions were God's impartial justice, but their flaming swords fell on Fallen necks ten times out of ten.

Celeste reached for the door, but Zeke was already moving down the alley. "This way's faster. Come on!"

They followed, Celeste's heart racing as her mind tried to catch up. Mariel, in the hands of the Virtues. How? Why? She didn't understand, but understanding didn't matter. Doing did. And what she needed to do was save her sister.

CHAPTER 3

PERDITION STREET WAS still shoulder to shoulder with all manner of masked merrymakers, but they pushed their way through. Around them people spilled from the saloons and brothels and opium dens into the street, drawn by the sight of the Virtues.

They were fearsome, dressed like the worst kind of avenging angels in a sensation story. They wore long white coats and small-brimmed felt hats, and they covered their faces with white porcelain masks that rendered them shrewd and inhuman even among the Aventum masqueraders. They sat astride silvered quarter horses and stared motionless at the crowd, all expression lost behind their pale facades.

"Look there," Zeke murmured.

In the center of the circle could only be the Order of Azrael. A single rider in white like all the others, but on his mask, tears red as fresh blood streaked porcelain cheeks. He held a flaming sword in one hand, the fire jumping and sparking like a living thing. Gleaming from its hilt was a chunk of golden divinity stone.

"That's no normal fire," Celeste said.

"Heavenly fire," Hypatia confirmed. "Powered by divinity. It can render a man to ash in seconds."

"A woman, too." She was thinking of Mariel.

A shrieking wail broke the silence, keen enough to shatter glass. Celeste recognized that voice, even in pain.

"Mariel!" She took a step forward, but Hypatia held her arm.

"Wait and see." Her voice was low with warning, and Celeste remembered Hypatia had tousled with the Virtues once before and had the thick, slicing scars down her back to prove it. Celeste looked again at that sword, and for a moment, she could almost feel the heat of it against her skin. Her eyes met the ones hidden behind the Azrael's mask, and she found herself looking away.

Sheriff Ybarra came out of the Eden, and the crowd parted for him. He wore a black dinner jacket and matching waistcoat with a white collared shirt, evidence he'd come from the mayor's affair. Ybarra was a regular fixture in town, a big-shouldered man fit for rounding up drunkards and settling disputes. He was nothing like the uncanny horrors of the Virtues. Celeste felt a touch of relief to see him, but his head was bowed, face hidden beneath his hat. The tin star pinned to his breast gleamed in the light of the Azrael's fiery sword.

"He won't look at the crowd with the Virtues around," Zeke observed, and any hope Celeste had of him fixing things sank like lead in her belly.

Mariel followed, half-collapsed between two Virtues, her bright red skirts dragging through the street. Her black curls had come undone and hung down her back, and something dark and sticky clung to her arms and hands.

Celeste moved before she could think, instinct calling her to her sister's side.

Zeke's arms clamped around her waist, pulling her back. "Steady."

"They mean to execute her!" she hissed. All she could think about was that flaming sword and heavenly fire at Mariel's neck.

"No, not in front of this crowd. Can't you feel it?"

He was right. The crowd was restless, muttering, unhappy that their hellish revelry had been ruined by this posse of God's men.

"What's she done?" someone shouted, and then the crowd picked it up.

"What's her crime, Sheriff?"

"Why the Virtues?"

"Leave her alone!"

The Virtues ignored them, pulling Mariel along before throwing her up onto the back of a horse to share a saddle with a masked rider. Her face was swollen and purpled, her nose and mouth bloodied, her head loose on her neck like she was stunned.

"They beat her." Zeke sounded dismayed, as if he hadn't quite believed it before he saw it, but Hypatia only snorted, experience telling her full well what kind of monsters they were.

The crowd was with Zeke, though, and their voices rose in indignation.

Celeste was shaking, and somehow her dagger was in her hand. What good it would do against a dozen armed men wearing masks, she had no idea. But she had to try something, didn't she?

"Steady, Celeste," Hypatia whispered in her ear. "And put that pigsticker away. You won't do her any good if they take you away, too. Let's see how this plays out."

Reluctantly, Celeste drew the blade back into its sheath.

Someone threw a bottle that shattered near the horses' feet. The riders struggled to control their suddenly skittish mounts. Sheriff Ybarra looked like he'd rather be anywhere else, but he came to the edge of the Virtues' circle, putting himself between them and the crowd.

"They're here at my request," he said, hands raised for calm. "There's a crime been committed, and they're the proper arresting body."

"What's she done?" Celeste cried. Hypatia may have wanted her to stay quiet, but she couldn't, not when they were about to take her sister away to who knew where. She was scared that if they rode away with Mariel now, she might never see her again. Her fear was not unfounded. Fallen had been known to disappear in Elect hands, only to show up headless in a ditch days later.

Ybarra scanned the crowd, pausing when he saw her. Goetia's permanent residents were small in number, especially those who were female and spent time dealing at the card tables. He recognized Celeste well enough.

"I'm not at liberty to share the details, but know that an innocent man is dead."

Disbelief rippled through the crowd. Goetia was as rough as any mining town, but murders were confined to the hard men who worked the mines or the darker haunts of Perdition. The Eden saw its share of brawls, but murder was still uncommon, and a murder that brought out the Virtues ten times as much.

"Who's dead?" Zeke shouted.

As if on cue, four Virtues came out bearing a body. It was wrapped in one of Hypatia's fine brocade curtains, but deep rust-colored stains had seeped through the silk, evidence of violence. They lifted the body up to another rider, who held it across his lap. Their expressions were lost behind their masks, but their straight backs and stiff movements betrayed their outrage.

"The dead is a Virtue," Ybarra said into the sudden quiet, his voice carrying. "That's why they've come. And the accused is a Fallen." He meant Mariel, and Celeste wanted to shout that her sister had a name, and someone who loved her, but what would Ybarra care? He spread his hands, as if the crowd had to understand his dilemma. As if there could be no other way.

"Will she hang?"

Celeste glared at the woman who'd asked it, an older Elect lady wearing costume devil wings.

Ybarra shook his head. "The Order of Chamuel will decide that, not me. Now, go on home and get some sleep. Leave justice to God."

He mounted his own horse, a modest bay, and gestured to the Virtues. As one, they turned their horses and cantered down Perdition, fading into the night, with the sheriff following. The last thing Celeste saw of them was the light of the Azrael's fiery sword.

"I'm going after them," she said, but even as she said it, she had no idea where they'd gone and no horse to get her there. The Virtues didn't loiter on Main Street or advertise a secret lair up in the mountains. Their comings and goings were mysterious, and since they kept their identities secret, it was hard to track them down.

Hypatia was thinking more clearly. "Go home, Celeste. I've got some favors I can call in. I'll find out where they've taken her and what comes next."

"What comes next?" she shouted. Her outburst drew eyes, but she didn't care. "You know better than anyone that if a Virtue has been murdered, they'll make someone pay, and that someone is going to be Mariel. That's what's next!"

Hypatia folded her arms over her chest, unmoved, but Celeste could tell by the way Hypatia chewed at her lip that she was worried.

"I've got to do something!" she pleaded. "Please!"

"I know you do." Hypatia's voice was calm, but there was a thread of fear there.

"Can't leave justice up to God," Zeke added morosely.

He and Hypatia exchanged a look. They knew as well as Celeste did.

God's justice always ended in blood.

CHAPTER 4

AT HYPATIA'S REQUEST, Zeke walked Celeste back to the ladies' boardinghouse where she and Mariel rented a room. He offered to sit with her in the parlor until they heard word from Hypatia, but Celeste was worried that Zeke's presence would only lead to questions from her landlady, so she declined. No doubt, Mrs. Ruth would find out about Mariel's arrest soon enough, but Celeste was hopeful she could find a few hours of sleep before facing her landlady's outrage over the scandal.

"Promise me you won't go rushing off to find Mariel on your own?" Zeke said.

"Of course." Celeste felt numb, as if all the life had been drained from her limbs. She mouthed the words she knew Zeke expected her to say, but she didn't know whether she meant them or not.

"Hypatia knows what she's doing," he said. "Give her time to work."

She nodded, ready to be away from him. Not that he'd done anything wrong, but if one more person told her to sit and wait, Celeste thought she might scream.

She looked up at him, his brown eyes so sincere. The telltale gold ring around his irises glistened, and to her surprise, tears rimmed his water line.

"We'll save her," he said. "I know we will."

"You're a good friend, Zeke." She touched his shoulder briefly and then retreated through the front door.

THE ELYSIUM STREET boardinghouse had once been the home of a wealthy Goetia mining family, but the husband had died and the wife had gone mad, murdering her children in one of the bedrooms on the fourth floor and then leaping to her own demise from the widow's walk above. Her paternal niece had inherited the house, declared it a home for single women, and promptly returned back East.

Insanity was one of the less-discussed side effects of mining divinity. Fallen were immune to it, but the Elect fell prey to the madness they called Abaddon's Revenge. Not often enough to dissuade those seeking to make their fortunes but common enough that it had a name and various tonics dedicated to its treatment.

Most Elect wouldn't set foot inside the boardinghouse due to its tragic past, which meant the women there were Fallen or the kind of women whom the polite society of the Elect had no use for—spinsters, sapphics, soiled doves. Celeste found their company a bonus rather than a burden. It was no exaggeration to say she preferred to spend her time with the damned, no matter what her blood might let her pass for.

Much of the house had run to just this side of shabby, but the parlor was still a grand affair. Brocaded wallpaper, leaded glass, and heavy mahogany wainscoting remained, befitting the grand place it once had been. The decor became noticeably worn as one moved farther into the house, and by the time one reached the rooms on the third floor where Mariel and Celeste lived, ornamentation was at a minimum. Plainly painted walls stripped of any wood or fabric that might have been resold for a profit were all that greeted her here.

She slid her key into a lock on a door that was hollow enough she could hear her neighbors coming and going whether she wished to or not. Once inside, she shut the door and secured the bolt. She was too anxious to make tea on the portable stove they kept for the kettle, so she simply sat at the table and waited.

She must have dozed off, because she woke to someone banging at her door. She rubbed her hands across her face, confused as to why she was sleeping in the kitchen chair, and then she remembered.

"Mariel," she whispered, and rushed to answer.

It was Hypatia. The woman looked the worse for wear, her normally jovial face haggard.

"Did you find her?" Celeste asked, waving her in.

Her nod was grim. She dropped onto the wooden chair on the other side of the kitchen table. "Do you have coffee?"

"Can't you just tell me?"

"Celeste, make me some goddamned coffee. I've been to hell for you, almost literally, and I think I earned it."

Celeste stiffened. "Sorry."

"And some for yourself, too," she said conciliatorily. "I think you will need fortifying."

She didn't like the sound of that. "I have tea. Will it do?"

"If by tea you mean hot water and whiskey, then yes."

Celeste rose and went to coax the burner on and place the kettle over the newly lit flame. She brought down the whiskey from the high shelf.

"The water will take time to boil. Tell me now. I can't wait."

Hypatia's exhale was long and expressive. "They have taken her to the Virtues' Circle."

"What is that? A thing? A place?"

"I reckon it's both. Some kind of special court where the Order of Chamuel presides."

The kettle whistled, and Hypatia sat silently as Celeste readied the tea. Once done, she brought the kettle, cups, and liquor to the table.

Hypatia took the whiskey first and drank straight from the bottle, her hand gripping the neck like a lifeline. Celeste watched, worried. Hypatia was a woman who liked her booze, but she'd never seen her so distraught. Whatever she had done to track the Virtues had left her shaken. Only after the alcohol had begun its work did she speak.

"She is at the territory courthouse, likely because there is a jail there in its cellar, carved out of the natural rock. They've got angelic wards around the exterior. What that means I don't quite know, but I was told it was important and breaking them would be costly."

"Told? By whom?"

She held up a hand, indicating that Celeste should let her finish. "Whatever they think Mariel did, they mean to hold her without interference. Those Virtues must want her real bad."

"So it's murder she's accused of, then." Part of her had been holding out for a misunderstanding, something more reasonable, but she couldn't deny the truth any longer.

The reality sat between them, heavy and undeniable now.

Celeste rested her face in her hands, overcome. "Heaven and hell, Hypatia. What do I do?"

"And here's the hard part."

She looked up, frowning. "Harder than Mariel arrested for murder?"

"I told you I'd call in a favor. Well, you might not like it, but he's offered to help."

"Who's offered to help? What are you talking about?"

"Abraxas."

"No." One word, dead as her heart. "Anyone but him."

Abraxas. Demon lord. A general in Lucifer's army, left behind when the minions of hell fell in retreat an eon ago, when the earth was still soft and new. Abraxas. Devil. Monster. And the only man she'd ever loved.

They had met at the Eden. He'd come that first time surrounded by the prettiest creatures she'd ever seen. A brown-skinned boy wearing velvet brocade, eyes like a cat under curling raven locks. A pale slip of a girl in silk. Wan, fey, and as pliant as a wilted flower. And another, neither boy nor girl, long-limbed, smooth-skinned, and made of fire and lightning and teeth.

"He owns their souls," Zeke had whispered as he and Celeste had watched from behind the bar.

"Thralls?"

He'd nodded. "What kind of person gives themselves to a demon?"

"A weak one," she'd replied.

In that moment, Celeste had thought herself better than those pretty playthings who trailed him, dogs waiting for their master's notice. Hubris, the ancients called it. It was an insult, to be sure, but it might as well have been a taunt. Celeste had made many mistakes in her life, but that one she regretted the most.

Abraxas's crimson eyes had turned to her.

Celeste did not believe in love at first sight then, and she still did not. But what she felt didn't have much to do with love, although that would come later. That night it was lust, pure and simple, although to call her feelings lust would be like calling a tornado a bit of a breeze. Desire roared through her, hungry like nothing she'd felt before, and she trembled.

"You okay?" Zeke's alarmed voice came to her, distant as the moon.

"No." She'd said it low and quiet, so maybe Zeke hadn't even heard her, but Abraxas had, and he'd uttered a quiet laugh that sounded like her ruin.

He'd come back the next night, that time alone, and sat at her table. She'd been so nervous that she lost too many hands and finally closed out. He'd smiled and asked her to dance, and that had begun their affair. It had lasted a season and ended in bitterness, she unable to give him what he wanted, which was everything, and he unable to settle for anything less. They had drawn battle lines and then retreated to a truce, and there they had both stayed until Hypatia had broken their uneasy peace.

"He's the one who told me about the Circle," Hypatia said, bringing Celeste back from her memories.

Celeste cleared her throat, trying to buy some time to settle her thoughts. "I can't believe you went to see him."

"He knows more about this town and the Virtues than anyone."

"He's dangerous, Hypatia. I should know. You shouldn't have done it."

"Dangerous to you, you mean."

"Dangerous to anyone."

"You and Mariel are like kin to me. I'd do it again if I had to, but it's not me he wants to see."

It took Celeste a moment to comprehend her meaning, only because she didn't want to. "Me?"

"I'm sorry, Celeste. I tried, you know I did. But it's you who's asking for help, so it's you he wants to see."

"You told him it was about Mariel?"

Her look was all sympathy. "Of course I did."

Celeste rubbed at her temples. "I don't know if that makes it better or worse."

"He said he'd help, but you don't have to go."

For a moment, Celeste clung to her words and the excuse in them. But it wasn't enough, and she knew it. "You said we were like kin, Hypatia, but do you have real kin?"

"You are my real kin. Everyone at the Eden is."

"I mean blood kin, like a ma and a pa. Brothers, sisters, cousins."

"A bushelful." She smiled at some fond memory. "So many, and all of them underfoot when I'm back home. Siblings and nieces and nephews. Heaven and hell, I came to Goetia to get a little breathing room."

Celeste folded her hands on the table, fingers gripping one another tightly. "I don't have any. Both our parents are dead, and good riddance. But we never had any extended relatives, at least none they told us about. It's just me and Mariel in all the world, and it pretty much always has been. All we got is each other, and I'd do anything to save her."

"I was worried you'd say that." She put her own hand over Celeste's. "He said he'd meet you at the crossroads on the edge of town, just past the tent city, where Perdition and Zion Street meet. He said before dawn."

It was still dark outside, but it wouldn't be for long. Celeste made herself stand. "I better go then, while the sun's still down, and I got the nerve."

She said it like that, but if she was honest, under all that fear was anticipation. To her dismay, she realized she missed him, and despite the way it had ended—the way she had ended it— she wanted to see him. She just wasn't sure why he'd agreed to this meeting at all. Abraxas never did anything out of kindness. He was a demon, after all. But whatever he wanted, even if it was only to hurt her, again, she would endure it.

"I'll walk out with you. And Celeste..."

She looked up, hoping for a last morsel of sage advice.

But all Hypatia said was, "I'm sorry."

CHAPTER 5

THERE WERE STILL a few Aventum stragglers on Perdition Street, but most had drunk their fill and found their beds. Clouds had moved in to blanket the mountains in a gloom, and the wind blew black ash down from the mine processing plants like tarnished snowfall. It made the air smell sweet, but it would eventually clog the roads and pile up on windowsills and rooftops, staining the city black until the next rain.

Detritus from last night's festivities littered the streets. Clumps of parade confetti and torn-down bunting from storefronts clogged the gutters, all of it quickly blackening with ash. Celeste spotted discarded paper handbills from the exhibition hall advertising strange new wonders made possible by divinity. Mechanical creatures of various shapes and sizes, giant clockwork claws meant to make the mines more efficient, even a newer and faster flying machine of some kind purported to cut the travel from Goetia to the capital by half.

She spied Taborite automatons sweeping the streets, uncanny golden skin and faceless heads gleaming in the lamplight. A gunshot sounded from behind, and she jumped, anxious as a hen. Some drunk was shooting at one of the mechanical sweepers, laughing as he peppered its gilded frame with bullets.

"Fool," she muttered, and hurried her pace.

The corner where Hypatia said the demon lord would meet her was deserted. To her right was the itinerant mining camp, no more than a cleared field where miners who could not afford four walls and a roof pitched their tents. It was a warren of twisting footpaths with no rhyme or reason, a dangerous sort of place populated by rough scrappers and heeled men looking for a fight. But now it slumbered, the workers given a day's reprieve on account of the Aventum holiday.

Celeste shivered and huddled deeper in her coat, black ash falling around her. Perhaps Abraxas wouldn't come, she thought, and she would be spared the torment of seeing him again. But that was a selfish desire, and one that brought on a mix of conflicting emotions. She reminded herself that she was here not for herself but for Mariel, so how she felt didn't matter.

There was a wooden post to her right with all manner of handbills nailed to its front. She read over them absently until one caught her eye. It was a solicitation for houses in the Drench, bought for cash and quickly. The purchasing party was to be contacted at the Tabor mine. Intrigued, she tore the bill from the post, reading more closely. She wondered what had happened to her childhood home in the Drench, the place where she'd spent her early years. She had never gone back—too many unpleasant memories lurked there—and surely another family had claimed it by now.

Abraxas appeared next to her as if he had been there all along and she had simply not been looking hard enough. He wore a long black coat, a brimmed hat, and a narrowly fitted jacket and trousers of deep midnight blue. His teeth flashed white against ink-dark skin.

"Celeste." He said her name like a prayer. Hushed, intimate, like she was something sacred. He leaned in close, and his lips brushed against her neck just below her ear. "Have you finally returned to me?"

She swallowed hard, fighting the desire that flooded her body. He smelled of rosewood and amber. If she closed her eyes, she could remember the taste of his mouth, cardamom and sin, and the rough heat of his hands as he unbuttoned her dress, palms sliding down her naked back.

It took all her willpower, but she stepped away, putting space between their bodies.

"I've only come to talk, Abraxas."

"Talk." He lingered over the word, lingered over her, his gaze appreciative. "What a pity."

She flushed, heat running up her neck and face. "It wasn't my idea to come to you. You should know that."

"Hypatia told me," he acknowledged, pacing around her like a giant cat evaluating his prey. "And yet here you are."

"Yes." She met his gaze, unflinching. He was long and lean, cut like a sliver of darkness had loosed itself from the night and formed into a man. Perfect and beautiful and dangerous. She shoved her trembling hands into her pockets and steadied her voice. "But there are rules, Abraxas."

A smile edged his mouth. "Rules? I did not agree to rules."

"I need rules, or I will not stay."

"Even for Mariel's sake?"

Her stomach dropped. He knew her too well. If this was how he wished to play, she was already damned. "This was a mistake." She turned to flee while she still could.

"Celeste. Wait." And now his voice was ordinary, or at least as ordinary as Abraxas could be. His words no longer brushed against her skin like silk, no longer conjured memories of seduction. "I will abide your rules. I would not have told

39

Hypatia to send you if I did not mean to help. But forgive me if seeing you again…" He exhaled. "It is not easy for me."

"This is not easy for me, either."

"You are the one who left me," he said, incredulous.

"Because you would have forced me to choose between you and Mariel. Because loving you meant losing my soul!" She matched his skepticism with a rising anger.

"Time passes, and the flesh fades. Forgive me for loving you so much that I wanted us to be together forever."

"By taking my soul?" she shouted in disbelief.

He growled incoherently and threw up his hands in frustration. She folded her arms across her chest, fighting the tightness around her heart. And there they were, back behind their battle lines.

Finally, Abraxas broke. "Let us walk," he offered, gesturing down the path. "You did not come here to renew old wounds."

She hesitated, distrustful of his change of tack.

"Not to worry. I'll return you safe and sound, and we will put our past aside for tonight. I know Mariel's life is at stake. I will be on my honor." He smiled, a slice of cold comfort. "How is that for a first rule?"

She gathered her purpose around her. He was many things, but he was not the kind to break his word. "It is a start."

They walked down Zion in the opposite direction of the camp. The road quickly succumbed to an old mining trail, the civilities of town giving way to a bitterly barren landscape. Cracked black earth, the remnants of lava flow, ran underfoot, and haphazard piles of black rock as tall as a man lined the thin path. Ash still sifted down around them, riding that ill wind, and it looked for all the world like Abraxas was leading her into some burned-out version of hell.

"I've never seen this road," she said, alarmed.

"Aventum Angelorum," he explained. "The earth plays tricks tonight. This was how it looked when it was an ancient battlefield. Here, demonkind battled the angelic choirs of seraphim until they were driven back to hell in retreat." His eyes touched briefly on the great mountain rising in the distance, and his tone turned bitter. "And there great Abaddon fell. And now they mine his body for their progress."

"You were with him. I remember you told me."

"I was." His shoulders bowed, and his gaze was distant, as if he saw the battle still.

"I forgot what this night meant to you," she admitted. "That you would be grieving."

"It's nothing." He shook himself free of the memory. "*Age quod agis.*"

"Latin?" It was a habit he had when he was contemplative. He had told her that it was because the old language was the closest to the demonic tongue, but she suspected he just liked the Roman philosophers.

He looked surprised that she'd remembered.

"I've missed hearing it," she admitted. It was a small concession, but she could see it pleased him.

"Tell me why you've come to me, Celeste Semyaza."

"Hypatia told you already."

"I want to hear it from you."

"Mariel is accused of killing a Virtue. They've taken her, and I'm afraid they will execute her tomorrow."

"Execute her, yes. Tomorrow?" His eyebrow rose. "Unlikely. What do you know of the Virtues?"

"Only what everyone knows."

"Then nothing."

She bristled at that, but it was true enough.

"The Virtues consider themselves men of exemplary

character," he continued, "the Order of Chamuel in particular, as they are arbitrators of the Almighty's own justice." He glanced at her, a wry smile framing his mouth. "They lie to themselves, as all righteous men do, but they will grant your sister a fair trial. Or, at least, what they see as fair. Else they fear themselves at risk of heavenly judgment."

"A trial? Not just an execution?" That was the first good news she'd heard. "With argument? And legal counsel?"

"She will have an advocate, yes, but it's not like you imagine it. Only heavenly law rules within the Circle, not the law of man. There is no arguing of the facts, only an examination into the accused's... spiritual fitness."

"She's Fallen." She was stating the obvious, but so was he. "They will consider her spiritually unfit by definition."

"And yet you think her innocent."

"I know she is innocent."

His smile stretched. "The Virtues are sanctimonious, but they make a fine point. If she is Fallen, she is sinful by fault. There is no innocence in her making."

She had begun to relax, the old familiarity of their relationship coming back. This was a man she knew well. His familiar stride beside her, the cadence of his speech, even the way he loved theological debate. It was the side of him that those who only knew him as a demon lord did not see. It was the part of him that had felt all her own.

"Have I ever told you about the baby bird?" she asked.

He tilted his head, listening. An invitation to continue.

"It must have been late summer, and I was probably nine, and Mariel five."

"A child Celeste," he murmured, amused. "You must have been a fierce thing."

"Not at all," she admitted. "I was as timid as a sparrow.

Mariel was the brave one. We still lived in the Drench back then, and a family of birds had built their nest in the eaves around the back of the house. Mariel wanted to see the babies, but I told her to leave them alone. I knew the mama could reject them if she smelled our touch on them. But Mariel didn't listen, curious as she was, and not five minutes later, she come up to me, all proud, and showed me that baby bird sitting in her hand."

"Alive?"

"She'd caught an older nestling, its plumage come in, and she was petting it. But she must have been too rough, because its feathers came off. She held it up for me to see, and I panicked, thinking for sure she'd ruined the poor thing. Well, she took one look at my face and burst into tears. The bird flew off, but it was still a baby, and it went careening down and crashed into the ground. Mariel didn't see it. She was wrapped up in my arms, wailing like it was the end of her world, asking me over and over again if I hated her. I said no, of course not, and told her it was just an old bird, and she needn't worry. But I was shaken. It was careless of her. She begged me not to tell Mama, so I didn't."

"And did the mother take the bird back?"

"The bird was dead. I don't know if Mariel had accidentally killed it before it fell to the ground or if she'd crushed it when she rushed into my arms, but after I'd taken her inside and calmed her down, I went back out and found its little body. I buried it out by the fence. I never told her she'd killed it. It would have wrecked her."

"I don't see how her killing a bird proves her innocent."

"How could a girl who cried over hurting a bird kill a man, much less a Virtue?"

"That was a long time ago, Celeste."

"It doesn't matter. People don't change, not the fundamental part of them. Mariel's a gentle soul. She didn't do it."

He stopped walking, and she was forced to stop with him. He studied her, gaze intense, not with the heat of seduction but with a careful kind of evaluation. Finally, he seemed to come to a decision.

"If you mean to confront the Virtues, you will need more than your Elect facade to pass through their careful watch. They will test you, no doubt."

"I know how to defeat their holy water. Zeke taught me the trick of it."

"Holy water will be the least of your worries."

"What, then?"

"Something they have created from divinity stone, mechanics, and angelic enchantments that probably they don't even understand, made from a remnant of the war not meant for human hands. Its subjugation is one of the few things demonkind truly fear."

He drew forth a pendant on a golden chain from around his neck. It held a single chip of divinity enclosed in a locket, and the locket was elaborately engraved with the sigils of hell.

"What is this?"

"Protection from the compulsion of the gloria."

"Gloria," she repeated. She took the protective locket and slipped it around her neck.

He said, "Go to the Circle and ask to speak to the head of the Order of Chamuel. You'll have to convince them of Mariel's innocence on your own. I cannot do that for you. The locket will keep them from devouring you whole, but the rest is up to you."

"Thank you, Abraxas."

His hand grasped her upper arm. "We aren't quite done," he

whispered, his voice smoke and silk.

Her pulse sped up. "What do you mean?"

"We've bargained tonight, have we not? Exchanged gifts."

She pressed her hand to the locket, confused. "You have given me a gift," she agreed, nervous, "but what have I given you?"

He closed the space between them, and she tilted her head up to meet him, as natural as breathing. She saw the curve of his satisfied smile just before she closed her eyes, and she did not care. She had missed him. Missed this.

This kiss was brief, just a promise of what could be, a reminder of what had been, and then it was over.

When she opened her eyes, she was alone.

CHAPTER 6

THE EARLY-MORNING sun was already breaking across the mountains by the time Celeste returned home. Her mind dwelled on her encounter with Abraxas, replaying his every word, looking for meaning in each gesture, lingering over that stolen kiss. But it was an indulgence, and one she could not afford. She had no doubt the Circle would waste no time conducting their sham trial. The fact that the crime for which Mariel was accused had happened in the middle of the night gave her some reprieve. The Order of Chamuel would have to round up their compatriots to convene the court. Celeste planned to confront the head of the Order of Chamuel before then, just as Abraxas had advised, and the only way to do that was to walk straight into the lion's den.

She stopped home only long enough to clean the ash from her coat and change into her best dress. She didn't know if a dress and a memory of who she used to be would be enough to convince the Virtue to talk to her, but they did serve as armor against her fears. The frock was a remnant of her time with her father, and in it, she resembled a woman of wealth and breeding. She was ashamed to admit there was comfort in it, but she would take courage from whatever she could.

The territorial courthouse stood on a hill overlooking the city. The locals called the place Golgotha on account of its lofty location and the tendency of those who passed through its halls to end up sentenced to death. It was a gruesome epithet for an institution meant to dole out justice, and it felt like an ill omen.

A crowd of lawyers, newspapermen, and the gawking curious loitered on the steps. Most were men, and she felt their eyes turn to her before she was halfway up the stairs. They moved aside, letting her pass, until she was at the grand entrance to the courthouse. Above the doors, a sculpture of the archangel Michael stared down at her in bas-relief, his flaming sword of justice raised high overhead. The avenging angel was a stark reminder of who she was and how much she, half-Fallen, did not belong within these hallowed walls. A sliver of doubt wedged its way through her careful armor and into her heart.

"*Fortis*, Celeste," she murmured to herself, Abraxas's Latin lingering on her tongue.

One deep breath, and she walked through the doors. She ducked under the arm of a man in a gray day suit who was arguing with the deputy guarding the entrance. She half expected the deputy to stop her or a ward to sound and reveal her subterfuge, but the lawman didn't even look up.

The noise rose by an order of magnitude inside. Attorneys, clerks, and men with badges packed the lofty space, going about the regular business of the court. Their voices echoed off the stone walls and marble floor, creating a deafening cacophony. She tried not to react to the aural assault as best she could, but it was impossible not to catch snippets of gossip as she passed.

"...murdered in bed..."

"...body mutilated..."

"...no doubt the wicked deed of that Fallen she-devil..."

She slowed at that last remark, realizing all the gossip was about Mariel. She tried to listen more, but the man who had said it, red side whiskers jutting from below his bowler hat, caught her looking. His eyes were a watery blue and narrowed in suspicion. Cold gripped the back of her neck like the touch of something sinister, and she quickly turned away.

Only to collide into the back of a woman.

"Goodness!" the stranger exclaimed, turning to face Celeste. She was young, surely no older than Celeste, and dressed in a daring unbustled skirt and shirtwaist with a smart black tie.

"Pardon." Celeste offered her a smile as apology.

The woman returned it, her quick eyes darting over Celeste. "Grace Walter," she said, introducing herself. "Reporter for the *Goetia Daily Howler*."

Celeste knew the *Howler*. It was one of the less reputable dailies in town, leaning more toward gossip and sensation than sober news, but she preferred it over the more staid *Herald*, so when Grace offered her hand, Celeste shook it.

"Celeste Anant." She used her father's name. At first, she had thought not to, but why shouldn't he be of use for once? Grace looked at her expectantly, as if all names were accompanied by occupations, so Celeste said, "I'm here about a legal matter."

"A law office secretary, are you? Well, I don't expect you'll get far with that today. All anyone can talk about is the Eden murder." She caught Celeste's frown and must have thought it something else, because she said, "Well, surely you've heard, although it did happen at an indecent hour, but you read the morning papers, don't you?"

Celeste thought to answer, but Grace pressed on, Celeste's participation in the conversation clearly not required.

"A Fallen woman murdered a Virtue. Order of Raphael, he

was, so practically a saint! Well, I don't know the details, but I know the sheriff was called in to break up a disturbance, and Ybarra walks right in and finds the girl covered in blood. Further investigation reveals a body, and then the Virtues are storming in and scooping her up before she can run." She gestured around the room. "We're all here to get the scuttlebutt. Oh, here's the clerk now!"

The noise in the room dulled to a muddled hush as a woman emerged from a side door carrying a large chalkboard. She climbed a stepladder to hang the board overhead from a hook on the wall. Every neck in the building bent back to read it.

The board was divided into neat columns filled with cramped, narrow handwriting. It listed the names of the accused, assigned judges, and courtrooms. A blank space at the end was reserved for the defendant's lawyer, assuming they had one.

Celeste read the board eagerly but failed to see Mariel's name.

Grace sighed in disappointment.

"What is it?" Celeste asked.

"This is today's docket, all the cases the court will hear. The Slaying Chanteuse isn't up there."

"Slaying Chanteuse?" Celeste repeated, alarmed.

"On account of her being a singer. Do you like it? I just thought it up. Or what about the Slaying Songbird? Yes, that has a bit more rhythm. Although it lacks the panache of the French."

"They're both terrible."

Grace shrugged, unconcerned. "Everyone's a critic. I'll find something to make the headline." She leaned in conspiratorially. "I hear the murder was a bloody one."

Her stomach turned. "How bloody?"

"You ever castrate a goat?"

She shook her head.

"Well, she castrated this old goat for sure." Grace laughed at her own joke and then added, belatedly, "Allegedly."

"How are they able to do it?"

"Castration? Well, with a sharp knife and a strong stomach, I suppose."

"No, the secret trial."

Grace laughed. "You must be new here. The Virtues are the real law in Goetia. Politicians, mining barons, clergy. It's a veritable who's who behind those masks. And with all that divinity at their fingertips, why, they do what they want, when they want to." She snapped shut the notebook she had been scribbling in. "Oh, they have certain rules to follow, like having a trial at all, but how honest can it be?"

"I've thought the same thing," Celeste murmured. "How do I get in to see the judge?"

"The Order of Chamuel?" The reporter gestured toward the far end of the room with a toss of her head. Celeste hadn't noticed it before through the crowd, but there stood a Virtue all in white, an olive branch painted across his white mask, guarding a door.

"Best of luck, but he won't talk to you," Grace said with a derisive snort. "He won't talk to anyone. Believe me. We've all tried."

Celeste's tone was grim. "He'll talk to me."

Grace cocked her head, eyes narrowing, as if seeing something new in the woman next to her. "What law office did you say you worked for, again?"

"I didn't." Celeste offered her a tight smile. "Thank you," she said, and walked away, the question unanswered.

Despite her professed optimism, once she was standing in front of the Virtue, doubt rushed upon her like a rising river. But she had thought about what to say on the walk over and was prepared.

51

"I need to speak to someone in the Order of Chamuel. I'm a witness to a crime, the murder last night. On Perdition. At the Eden." She was stumbling over her words, nervous as a virgin in a whorehouse. But why wouldn't she be, having witnessed a murder? She started again. "I'm here to speak to the Virtue in charge."

The Virtue was still as granite and as cold. She repeated herself, with the same lack of results. But she refused to give up. She was about to inquire yet again when the Virtue moved. Behind him was an elaborately carved door with the now-familiar flaming sword upon it. He opened the door and then stepped aside, waving for her to enter.

She expected to see another room or a hallway but instead faced a lacy metal gate and, behind it, a box. The box looked big enough to fit three grown men, and it was connected to a series of visible ropes and pulleys. She glanced down through the grate at the bottom of the box, and there, far, far below, glowed a golden chunk of divinity.

She had never ridden in an elevator but knew this to be one, and the divinity below must be the beating heart of the mechanism that moved it.

She looked back briefly toward the courthouse lobby. Grace Walter met her gaze, her mouth open in shock.

"Step all the way in, Miss." There was a man just inside dressed in a simple coat and trousers. Short in stature and thin as a settler's soul, his hands rested on the lever that worked the machine. Celeste hesitated at the threshold, unsure, until the man looked up. Golden rings wreathed his brown eyes.

It was enough to move her forward.

Once she was inside the elevator, the Virtue pulled the metal gating closed and shut the outside door. The Fallen man pulled his levers, and the box filled with the sound of mechanics, whirling and cranking. The divinity below flared, bright as a flash of the infinite. They lurched upward. Celeste gripped the railing, knuckles white.

The elevator operator chuckled. "Don't you worry none, Miss," he said. "This here machine is in apple-pie order. I maintain it myself. You're safe as can be."

"And where does it go?" she asked, struggling even to find that many words as the box shuddered ever higher.

"Why, this one?" The old man laughed, loud and a little mad. "This one runs between heaven and hell."

CHAPTER 7

AFTER THAT, THEY rode the elevator in silence, and she was grateful for it. The man was unsettling, and by the time the machine came to a halt, she was more than willing to face whatever was before her rather than spend another moment in that stifling box.

He opened the gate and then the outside door and gestured her out. No sooner had she crossed to solid ground than she was confronted with another olive-branch-marked Virtue. This one was not alone. Beside him stood two more Virtues, their masks weeping bloody tears. One held in his hand a small silver bowl, the other iron shackles.

Sweat broke out at the back of her neck. She felt her knees shake and locked them in place. Behind her, the Fallen man giggled.

She forced herself to calm and asked, "What's this?"

"Place your hand in the bowl."

"Why must I?"

"If you wish to pass through, you must take the test."

"But what does it do?"

"It is holy water."

Holy water to burn the flesh. She tilted her face up to show him her ringless eyes. "I'm no Fallen." The lie came smooth to her tongue.

He leaned in, using his superior height to great effect. "Then you have nothing to fear." She could not see his smile behind his mask, but she knew it to be there. His next words crawled across her scalp like a nest of spiders. "Do not despair. Should you fail, the Virtues have ways to rehabilitate your kind."

She glanced at the man with the shackles as she worked her fingers inside her gloves. Zeke had assured her his defense against holy water would work, but now, standing here with no way out, she was terrified. Even though she had committed no crime, she understood her very existence was crime enough to the Elect. The Fallen were the embodiment of disobedience to God's will, to a well-ordered and God-fearing society. They were a reminder of everything that could not be controlled, and the fact that they had talents and abilities the Elect did not, not just in spotting the mining lode but in beauty and art and myriad other ways, only drove the hate deeper. She did not doubt this Virtue would delight in being her judge, jury, and executioner.

But Celeste had come this far, so with a steady tug, her eyes not leaving the Virtue's, she pulled the glove from her left hand.

She dipped her fingers into the water.

The Virtue's eyes watched, almost hungry. When nothing happened, he grunted in what sounded like disappointment.

She did her best to keep her face straight but could not help the small sigh of relief that tripped from her lips. She withdrew her hand, carefully shook the water from her fingers, and slipped her hand back into her glove, hoping the Virtue did not see how badly it shook.

The second Virtue stepped forward. He uncurled his fingers.

On his palm sat a small mechanical cicada. It was beautiful, its wings like delicate lace, its eyes chips of gold divinity.

"Place it on your tongue," the first Virtue commanded.

"That won't be necessary," a masculine voice called from farther down the hall. "Let her pass."

The man holding the cicada paused, clearly contemplating whether he must obey the order. She could not see his face, but she knew something dark stirred in his heart. His eyes behind the mask lingered on her lips, and she slapped a hand over her mouth, taking a step back.

The voice came again, this time more urgent. "I said, let her pass!"

Resentment rippled between the Virtues, but all three stepped aside. Before her, down a short hallway, was yet another door. It stood ajar, and the voice that had saved her from the mechanical insect had come from within.

"Come, Miss. Please. They won't harm you."

"They wish to!" she shouted.

The first Virtue, the one who had threatened her with "rehabilitation," shifted on his feet, and she knew it to be true.

"But they won't," the voice said. "I have commanded it, and to disobey me is to disobey the law of heaven."

Now they retreated in truth, unwilling to cross the man behind that door.

She made herself move.

Something brushed against her scalp, and she glanced back to see one of the Virtues from the Order of Michael pulling his hand back. Had he touched her hair?

She shuddered and hurried her pace.

She passed through the open door and entered, half expecting to find a monster. But instead, she found only a man, distinguished silver hair parted down the middle and curls cropped just below his ears. He had a great beard and thick chop whiskers that covered his cheeks.

He was seated behind a wooden desk at the far end of a room decorated in Persian rugs and stuffed with finely bound books in bookcases. She spied works on magic and theology and an entire shelf devoted to the study of the Fallen. A fire blazed in a small fireplace in the corner, creating a stifling heat, but the inviting armchairs before the hearth looked like the perfect place to spend a cozy afternoon, not to interrogate innocents.

The whole place, man and books and fire, were not what she had expected. The dissonance made her stumble over a nonexistent fold in the rug.

He looked up at the noise. He had been writing at his desk with an old-fashioned quill, the pot of ink at his elbow and parchment before him. When he saw her, he smiled.

"You must be the sister."

She froze in surprise, unsure what to do.

"Sheriff Ybarra told me to expect you."

Of course. The sheriff had seen her in the crowd. Of course he would expect her to come. All her subterfuge was pointless.

"So you know I am Fallen."

"The sheriff did mention it, yes." He gestured to a hard-backed chair in front of his desk. "Sit. Please. And forgive me for the matter at the door. The gloria was extreme."

The gloria? The metal cicada had been the thing Abraxas had warned her about? The thing even demonkind feared?

"I do apologize for that," he continued, "but the holy water, well, I have long suspected the Fallen had a way of outsmarting the holy water. It's quite outdated as a means of discerning Fallen ancestry. I know your kind are quite clever."

"My kind?" Her voice was thick with disdain, but the man continued on blithely.

"Will you tell me how you did it?" he asked, eager. "Defeated the holy water?"

She kept her mouth closed, but her fingers flexed within her gloves, the wax covering them cool and solid.

He waited a moment, but when it was clear she had no intention of speaking, his shoulders slumped in disappointment. "Perhaps another time," he said.

"I've come to talk to the head of the Order of Chamuel about my sister. Is that you?"

"I am Mr. Ibrahim, head of the Order of Chamuel." He inclined his head. "At your service."

She frowned. "You have a name?"

"Most people do."

"I mean, that you would share with me."

"Of course."

"I thought the Virtues were particular about their anonymity."

He smiled at her like she was a child who had expected the closet to be full of monsters and opened it only to find her mother's fancy dresses. "I don't know what you've heard about the Virtues, but I assure you, we are not what you think."

"I *think* you are holding my sister."

"Ah… Yes, I'm afraid that is true."

"I want her freed."

"We both know that's impossible."

"But she's innocent."

He leaned back in his chair, hands templed as if in prayer. The leather seat creaked under his weight. "Everyone claims they are innocent. Do better."

"What?" It was a strange thing for him to say, and she was not sure what he meant.

"Do. Better." He enunciated each word as if she were a dolt. "Offer me a better defense."

Celeste was quick with a knife but not nearly as quick with her words, particularly when faced with an Elect man watching her as if waiting for her to perform a carnival trick. But she felt a possibility opening before her, and she would not waste it.

"I heard the slaying was violent," she offered. "Bloody."

The corners of Ibrahim's eyes tightened as if she had poked a finger into a fresh wound. "Salacious gossip. Tongues already wagging, I see."

"Is it true?"

"It was not a gentle death," he conceded.

"My sister is a woman of small stature. She was easily subdued by your Virtues. And yet someone held down a grown man and emasculated him. Does this sound like a crime she could commit?"

He nodded encouragingly, as if he were a law professor and she his student. It was like being in her father's house again, and bile rose in the back of her throat, but she continued, determined to pass whatever test this was.

"And what would be her motive for something as gruesome as murder?" she continued. "She is a songstress. What business would she have with a Virtue? Whereas I am sure you truck with dangerous and powerful men, Mr. Ibrahim. Isn't it much more likely that one of those men is responsible for this terrible crime? Have you even begun to look among your own class, or are you content to let an innocent girl who happens to be a Fallen be your scapegoat?"

As she spoke, the cadence of the Elect came back to her. Even as the words poured eloquently from her mouth, a strange horror accompanied them, as if she were watching herself at a distance. *Hypatia was right*, she thought to herself. *I am one of them.* A shiver of self-loathing lodged in her chest.

The smile Ibrahim had held fixed on his face broke into a

grin. "Impressive, Miss Semyaza, although the accusation at the end was a bit dramatic. But I see you have a mind for logic."

"You expected less of a Fallen?" she asked.

"I expected less of a woman."

The dismissal in his voice rocked her back. It took her a moment to recover, but recover she did. "Then you are a fool, Mr. Ibrahim, plain and simple."

She thought for a moment she had gone too far, but Ibrahim clapped his hands together, laughing. "Excellent, excellent." He leaned forward. "And I cannot argue with you. My wife says I'm hardheaded." He templed his fingers again. "You make a convincing argument on your sister's behalf, Miss Semyaza, but you make it to the wrong person."

She sighed, sour with disappointment. "To whom should I be making it?"

"You know your sister will go to trial."

"The Virtues' Circle."

"Precisely! So tell me. What do you know of the Circle?"

"I know it is a secret court."

"A court with a judge, an *accusator*, and an *advocatus diaboli*." He counted the three roles off on his fingers. "I'd like you to be Mariel's *advocatus diaboli*."

Was that his motive for her performance? "Shouldn't that be the job of a lawyer?"

"No, not here. We are not that kind of court. We speak with a plain heart before God. None of the chicanery of man, hiding behind rules meant to obstruct the facts. We seek only the truth."

Abraxas's "spiritual fitness".

"You would free my sister, if I were to convince the judge of her innocence?"

He pointed heavenward. "If we did not, God himself would strike us down."

"Even though she… even though *we* are Fallen?"

"Aren't all of us God's creation, even the Fallen? Would not God have taken Lucifer back but for the angel's pride?"

She was not as certain as Ibrahim on the matter of Lucifer's wishes or God's forgiveness, but she'd already pushed her good fortune as far as she dared, so she kept her theological opinions to herself.

He folded his hands across the desk. "Well? Do you accept the role of *advocatus*?"

"What is required of me?"

"Only what you've already demonstrated. A passionate defense of your sister. You can present that as you wish. But truly, the only thing that is necessary is that you speak the truth in your heart. And wear a gloria when you do it."

She swallowed, queasy at the thought of putting the mechanical bug on her tongue. Her hand moved to touch Abraxas's pendant, but she stopped herself, forcing her hands together in her lap instead. "And how do I know the judge will listen to me? How will I know you will be honest and fair?"

"Miss Semyaza, we are sworn in service to the archangels and to God himself. The judge would risk eternal damnation should he sentence an innocent woman to death. Surely that is enough to ensure the Circle's integrity."

It was a trap. She knew it as well as she knew her own heartbeat, as well as she recognized a cheat sitting at the faro table, but oh, it was baited so sweetly. What could she do? If she said no, it would be as if she had decided her sister was unworthy of her defense. But if she said yes…

She could almost feel the jaws of the shackles closing around her leg, the cold edge of iron biting into her skin. She could hear Abraxas's warning not to trust the Virtues, that righteous men had a way of lying to themselves.

"I accept."

Ibrahim clapped his wrinkled hands together. "Splendid." He turned the parchment on his desk toward her and proffered his quill. "If you will sign here—as Semyaza, mind you, although Anant may be appended—I can take you to see Mariel."

"Just like that?"

His teeth when he smiled were yellow and small. She hadn't noticed them before.

"Yes, Miss Semyaza. Just like that."

CHAPTER 8

THEY TOOK THE elevator down to hell.

Abraxas had told Hypatia there was a jail below the courthouse where they would be holding Mariel. But as the elevator rattled past the basement level, she realized there were secret tunnels carved into the foundational rock on which Goetia had built its hall of justice.

As they descended, so did the light, until the only illumination was a divinity-powered lamp Ibrahim held high to hold back the darkness.

"How far down does this go?" She had not meant to ask, but she could feel the weight of the place, the press of thousands of tons of stone all around them.

"Almost there," he answered, unperturbed.

"And you are keeping my sister down here?" There was a hysterical edge to her voice that she could not hold back.

He glanced at her. The lamp turned his features ghastly, creating shadows in the hollows of his cheeks and eyes. "We keep all our Fallen down here."

"If the gloria can compel someone to tell the truth, why not simply give one to my sister and let her tell you she is innocent?"

"We do not compel the accused to confess. It is distasteful. And glorias are not infallible. There are complications in their use, for example, if the confessor truly believes their lie. The gloria cannot counter sincere belief."

Abraxas had not mentioned that, and she wondered if he knew.

The elevator lurched to a stop, and he opened the cage and motioned her forward. "Did you know this was once a mine?" He closed the elevator door and nodded to the lift man. "Not a very profitable one. The lode was small and quickly mined to depletion. When they built the courthouse here, they found better uses for these tunnels."

They walked past cells carved into the rock, all blessedly empty. Although once she thought she saw something move deep in the bowels of one of the foul cages but could not be sure. Finally, they came to a stop. Mr. Ibrahim fiddled with a sconce on the wall, and a lamp came to life, casting a soft white glow in a wide swath around them.

"You keep her in the dark?" she asked, outraged.

"The Fallen do not need light." He said it with the confidence of one who had studied a people from afar but never shared a dinner table with them.

"Of course she needs light."

His gaze cut to Celeste, doubtful. "Even so, divinity remains in the walls. It casts enough light by which to see."

The walls beside her were black and empty. "There is no divinity here. You yourself said this place is depleted!"

He looked surprised. "I was told as much by the prisoners but thought them liars." He studied her in the lamplight. "I believe you are the first Fallen who has ever been down here who was not a prisoner."

Words like "monstrous" and "barbarity" rose to her lips, but before she could utter them, a voice spoke from the cell before them.

"Celeste?"

She turned. "Mariel?"

Mariel emerged from the darkness, ragged and damaged, birthed back to Celeste like a once-discarded goddess. She was still beautiful—nothing could dull that—but her raven hair was tangled and wild around her brown face, and her once-fine Aventum dress was torn and filthy. A massive welt purpled her cheek.

She held a hand across her golden-ringed eyes, blinking in the light.

"Oh, Mariel!" Celeste rushed to her, but there were bars between them. She pressed her hands forward and was able to touch her palms to her sister's, twine their fingers together.

Celeste smiled, trying to convey a half dozen feelings at once.

Mariel wept, tears cutting streaks down her unwashed face. "Get me out of here," she hissed.

"I'm working on it." Celeste squeezed her fingers once before letting go and turning back to Ibrahim. She channeled all her remembered Elect entitlement and said, "What is the meaning of this? No light, no food, no medical care? You purport to believe that we are all God's children, but you have treated my sister as no more than an animal."

The Virtue pursed his lips but said nothing.

"She is innocent until judgment," she continued. "You said so to my own ears. Or are you a hypocrite, Mr. Ibrahim? A member of an order that calls itself just but would treat a woman like—"

"Enough, Miss Semyaza." His voice was quiet, but his words had sharp ends. "You have made your point. I will fetch a doctor."

"And food and clean clothes and—"

He lifted his hand, palm forward, and now his voice showed his irritation. "Do not push my goodwill."

She folded her owns hands at her waist so that he would not see that they were shaking. "Now. Please."

His gaze swung between them before he finally turned on his heel and walked back to the lift. She watched as he went beyond the circle of light from the wall sconce, his lamp bobbing off into the darkness like a firefly cast from the swarm. Mariel made a sound as if to speak, but Celeste held a finger to her lips, begging silence. The metal clank of the elevator door echoed down the old mining shaft, and then came the whirl of the machinery, and she knew they were alone.

Celeste fell to her knees before the cell, pressing her hands against the bars again. Mariel mirrored her, and for a moment they sat in silence together.

"We haven't much time," Celeste said, breaking the spell of grief. "He'll be back soon enough. Tell me what happened."

"Get me out," Mariel repeated. "It's cold and dark, and there's something down here in one of the cells that doesn't want me here."

"I will, but I need to know what happened."

Mariel released her sister's hands and sat back, legs drawn up, arms around her knees. Her face was closed, and for a moment, it was as if Celeste was looking at a stranger.

"Mariel," she said softly. "Tell me."

Mariel seemed to gather herself, and finally, she spoke. "I had finished singing, you know the one." She cleared her throat and sang: "*No wedding feast was spread that night, two graves were made next day… one for the little baby, and in one the father lay…*"

Celeste nodded. It was a dreary tune, but Mariel loved it, and her pure soprano soared, even in this awful place.

"Hypatia told me I was done for the night, so I went to the back room to rest."

"Zeke said you weren't feeling well."

Her eyes cut away for a moment. "That's right. So I lay down to sleep, and when I awoke, there was a dead man next to me." She ran an unsteady hand across her face. "Oh, Celeste, there was blood everywhere. More blood than I'd ever seen. More blood than I thought a man could hold! And I was covered in it." She spread her dark-stained dress wide. "I still am," she whispered.

"But who was he? How did he get there?"

Mariel shook her head.

"You slept through it all?"

She dug a finger through a rip in the fabric of her skirt. "I may have had a nip of the laudanum Hypatia keeps for sore throats."

Celeste bowed her head. "You were intoxicated."

"I was asleep," her sister protested. "And don't start your moralizing with me. It was one time."

"All right." Celeste doubted it was one time, but there was no use arguing it now. "Can you remember anything else?"

"Is not waking up to a dead body in the bed with me enough?" Mariel dropped her forehead to her knees. "I must have been in shock, because the next thing I knew, I was surrounded by those white villains."

"The Virtues. Do you remember anything else? Was there someone else in the room when you woke?"

"I don't know! I don't remember!"

"It's okay," Celeste soothed. "I'm only asking."

Mariel looked up at her through her hair. "So you believe me?"

"Of course."

She sniffed, wiping roughly at her face. "Do you think you can make the Virtues believe me?"

Above them, machinery rumbled to life. The elevator was coming back.

"I'm going to try, but listen, Mariel. Why do you think they named me your *advocatus*?"

Her brow furrowed in confusion. "Because you're smart and honest."

It was nice to hear it, but Celeste knew the truth. "Because Ibrahim thinks I will fail."

"I don't understand."

"Look around you, this place you're in. They would not treat you this poorly if they ever expected you to walk free again. Imagine the scandal, to treat you like this."

Mariel stared at Celeste, her words penetrating.

"And who am I?" Celeste continued. "A young woman untrained in the law, which Ibrahim assures me won't matter. He takes me for a fool, or worse, a dog performing an impressive trick."

"I—I don't understand."

"He's playing some kind of game. One I haven't quite unraveled yet. But I know a man looking to cheat when I see one, and Ibrahim is as sharp as they come. But he's underestimated me, Mariel. Underestimated us. As all men do. And we'll make him pay for it."

The boom of the elevator coming to a stop reverberated. Celeste peered down the corridor to see Ibrahim's lamplight disengage from the darkness and move their way.

"And I have help. Hypatia, and…" She hesitated, unsure whether to tell her about Abraxas. She was not sure Mariel would appreciate the demon lord's involvement, even if it was to her benefit. Celeste settled on "another benefactor. We will get you out of here. That I promise. I won't leave you to the Virtues' mercies."

As Ibrahim's footsteps came closer, Celeste stood, straightening her clothes and dusting the dirt from her hands. Accompanying him were two more Virtues. One held a medicine bag and bore the rod of healing that marked him as from the Order of Raphael. The other carried a jug of water and a bowl of something that smelled like gruel.

"I've brought the things you requested," Ibrahim said. His bushy gray eyebrow arched upward, and he winked. "I trust that gave you ample time to talk privately, as I assume you intended?"

Celeste moved away from the cell, lowering her voice. "When will her trial be held?"

"High noon of the third day. So that gives you a little less than forty-eight hours to gather your thoughts."

"But if I am to interview witnesses, gather evidence, surely that is not enough time."

"What evidence is there to gather when the Circle asks you only to speak from your heart?"

"Of course. But—"

"That is the nature of the appointment, Miss Semyaza. If you do not think yourself up to the task, it is not too late for me to assign it to one of my brethren."

"No." She made herself take a deep breath and resettle. "I will do it."

The doctor produced an iron key and opened the cell. For a moment, there was nothing between the sisters, and Celeste took a step forward. Then the Virtue holding the jug moved between them, his body blocking the way, and the moment passed.

"I'll see you out now, Miss Semyaza," Ibrahim said. "I'm sure you have plenty of work to do and, as you know, little time in which to do it."

CHAPTER 9

She had stayed longer in the courthouse and its underground jail than she realized, and by the time she reemerged, afternoon sunlight streaked the lobby floor. The crowd of lawmen and reporters had finished their day's work and retired elsewhere for supper or other entertainments. Only a handful of clerks remained, walking to and from their offices, talking to each other in hushed tones, as if they were in a cathedral and law was holy work. Golden Taborites trailed the clerks like obedient children, their mechanical arms piled with boxes and folders and the business of meting out man's justice.

Now that she was *advocatus*, she wanted to return to the Eden to see the scene of the crime for herself, no matter how gruesome. She believed there were clues to be found there that would help Mariel's cause. No matter how Ibrahim insisted the Circle wished only to hear of the purity of Mariel's soul, she knew evidence of her sister's innocence would be the only thing to save her.

But first, Celeste had someone else to call upon.

Miss Grace Walter was in the act of closing the *Howler*'s office for the day, but Celeste convinced her to stay longer so they could talk. Soon Grace was listening, enthralled by what Celeste had to say. When she concluded her tale, Grace clapped her hands in delight.

"Can you print it?" Celeste asked, worried that she might find her story lacking.

"Can I?" Grace grinned. "Will the front page do?"

They promised to speak again should Celeste have any other headline news, and the two parted ways just as the sun slipped behind the mountains. Up on the slopes, Celeste could see the divinity lights of the mines shining against black peaks.

With the night only starting and the hangover of Aventum lingering, Perdition Street was a shadow of itself. It would take another few hours for the saloons, gambling halls, opium dens, and bordellos to lumber back to life, particularly after the holiday. But live again they would. In other parts of the territory, a growing temperance movement had already dampened the excesses of good living, but here where the lords of hell had touched the earth and their children still made habitat, nothing could quite curb the *sin* of it all.

Despite the rowdy reputation Hypatia prized so dearly, the Eden stood among its lesser siblings on Perdition like the pride of the litter. Only the Excelsior Hotel and the opera house on the respectable side of town rivaled it in dignity. It was a massive three-story building built of rare white brick, wood, and iron. Its arching front windows and three-columned portico were trimmed in Goetia cement, the limestone cut through with divinity dust. Divinity also powered the lights, both outdoors and those illuminating the brightly painted walls inside.

Hypatia had fashioned the Eden after the ancient city of Alexandria. Columns of pink granite rising from floor to ceiling, tiles of sea blue paving the bottom of an indoor fountain, and a ceiling tiled in gold tin as bright and warming as the Mediterranean were the Eden's most noticeable features. Beyond the decor were the betting tables and the ace-high spirits, watered down though they might be. And then there was the entertainment. Every saloon along Perdition offered music of some sort, popular waltzes or ragtime, and many offered dancing, couples with dance cards on Thursday night and ladies with knee-baring skirts on Saturdays. But only the Eden had a songstress like Mariel. They all knew she was good enough to sing at the opera house or in the concert halls of the great cities, but she was Fallen, and the Fallen stayed in Goetia, close to the mines.

As Celeste approached the Eden, she spotted a Virtue standing guard at the door. The windows showed the interior dark and empty. She kept walking, hoping to avoid the Virtue's notice, and had just passed out of his view when a figure in the shadows waved her down.

It was Hypatia, and she held a finger to her lips, motioning Celeste to silence. They melted into the shadows in the alley, away from the Virtue's watch.

"Damn Virtues turned me away from my own establishment." Hypatia was mad enough to turn milk. "Said it's closed until I get the place cleaned up properly."

"Can you still get in?"

"It's my place, ain't it? I won't allow no Virts to keep me from what's mine."

"Can you get me in?"

"'Course. But why?"

Celeste quickly explained about the meeting with Ibrahim and her new role as Mariel's defender. Hypatia gave her a long look that Celeste couldn't quite decipher, then motioned for her to follow her around back.

"And what about your meeting with Abraxas?" Hypatia asked as they walked. "He didn't hurt you, did he?"

She sighed. "Not the way you mean it."

"It never is." She gave her a sideways look, urging her to say more, but Celeste wasn't up for discussing it.

They arrived at the back door, retracing the very steps they'd taken in the dark hours of the morning.

Hypatia raised an eyebrow. "Wager they left it unguarded?"

"They can't be that dense."

"Arrogant is more like it." Hypatia tried the door. No guard came rushing to investigate the noise, but it had been bolted from the inside. She fished around under a loose brick and pulled out a flat ruler. She wedged it into the space between the door and the frame. It took her a few tries, but with a powerful heave, she threw the bolt free. "I've locked myself out a few times," she admitted, before she quietly opened the door.

Moonlight streamed in through the front windows, but they were careful to stay low as they passed the bar and went back toward the interior hallway.

"Do you know where it happened?" There was no need for Celeste to specify what she meant by "it."

"I know where they drug him out from." Hypatia looked down pointedly. Bloodstains colored the carpet like the trail to the witch's house in a dark fairy tale. They followed the blood until it ended at Hypatia's office.

The door was ajar. Hypatia lit a lamp on a desk strewn with papers. Light suffused the room, revealing a sleeping cot and shelves stuffed with what looked to be records, order forms, and the various sundries of running a business. Much of it was covered in dried blood. The bed in particular was soaked through with it. Celeste remembered Mariel saying there was blood everywhere, more than she thought a man could hold.

"Start looking," she said, grimly setting to the task.

"For what?"

"A clue."

"Being a mite more specific might help."

"A murder weapon."

"Celeste, if there was a knife here big enough to do this kind of damage to a body, don't you think it would have been found by now?"

"Then look for something else. Signs a killer was in here. Footprints, secret papers... Hell, I don't know. Anything that might help Mariel."

Hypatia looked dubious but got to work, shuffling through the papers on her desk.

Celeste lifted the corner of the mattress, the bedding stiff and sticky, and peered underneath. There was nothing there. She moved to the nearest bookshelf, reading across the spines of tomes, looking for she knew not what.

"What's this?" Hypatia murmured. She held up a handbill, the same one Celeste had noticed at the crossroads, the one about wanting to buy Drench houses.

"I've seen this before," she said, taking it and looking it over.

"Could be a clue," Hypatia offered.

"Or it could be trash. These seem to be everywhere in town." She stuffed the bill into her coat pocket.

They continued to search, but after a quarter of an hour, they had turned up nothing suspicious or out of place.

"This is no good." Frustration bubbled in Celeste's gut. She stepped back, trying to imagine it as Mariel had told it, with her lying on the bed asleep.

"What are you doing?" Hypatia's voice rose.

"I'm lying down." Celeste took the position Mariel must have had and tried not to think about the grisly sheets against her back. "Come lie next to me."

"Why?"

"Mariel said she awoke with the dead man in the bed with her,

77

but by my reckoning, there's not room for that." She extended her arm, and it dangled off the edge.

"Two don't fit," Hypatia agreed. "I can tell that from experience."

Celeste sat up, scooting off the side. "Have you been bringing your saloon girls in here?"

Hypatia grinned. "Only for kissin'. For more serious stuff, I take 'em upstairs to my boudoir."

"The mattress was soaked through, which suggests he was killed here."

"It is a lot of blood." Hypatia scratched at her neck, thinking. "Do you know how he died?"

"Castration. Bled out."

"Heaven and hell," she murmured. "That sounds personal."

"How could he have entered alive, been castrated on this bed too narrow for two, and all the while Mariel slept through it?"

"This might do it." Hypatia picked up a laudanum bottle from the desk and shook it. It was empty.

"If she drank that whole bottle, she would be dead."

"Maybe it was already half-empty?"

Celeste frowned. "Wouldn't you know? I mean, isn't it yours?" Mariel had said Hypatia gave her the laudanum.

"I've never seen this bottle in my life." Hypatia reached for something else on the desk and lifted up the remains of a broken cap seal. "Freshly opened in this room."

"Then someone else must have been here to share the bottle."

"The victim?"

"Or the murderer." Celeste shook her head. "It makes no sense."

Hypatia's face was troubled.

"What is it?"

"There's one way it makes sense." Her look was sympathetic.

"Mariel's not telling you the truth."

A noise in the hallway, and a figure popped up in the doorway. She was short, her black hair cut in a fringe. Her expression was serious, so Celeste couldn't see her dimples, but she was sure this was Hypatia's new girl, Lilitha.

"Virtues are coming," she hissed. "Four of 'em. They're at the front door."

Hypatia cursed, and they moved, running fast down the hallway, careful not to make any more noise than they had to. They were out the back door, pulling it shut, when they heard voices from the front.

"Go!" Hypatia said, pushing them up the back stairs that led to her private rooms. They pounded up the steps, quick as they could, and didn't stop to breathe until they were on the other side of the apartment door.

Celeste collapsed onto the nearest chair, heart hammering in her chest. Hypatia followed suit, falling onto her settee and motioning for the woman who had warned them to join her. Lilitha snuggled up next to her boss, eyes bright.

"That was exciting!" the saloon girl said.

"Too exciting," Hypatia said. "My old heart's not meant for exercising anymore."

Lilitha ran a finger down Hypatia's ample cleavage. "Oh, I think your heart's holding up just fine."

Face flushed, Hypatia giggled like a schoolgirl and leaned in for a kiss.

"Could you not?" Celeste pushed herself to her feet and stomped into the kitchen. There was a pitcher of water out, and she poured herself a glass.

She heard Lilitha mutter, "Why's she got a stick up her backside?" and Hypatia reply, "Shhh, love. Her sister's facing Azrael's sword. She's had a day of it. Be kind."

"A day of it" was an understatement. Between having her sister arrested by Virtues, meeting with Abraxas, confronting the head of the Chamuels, and finding nothing at the murder scene but the fact that Mariel liked laudanum more than she'd let on and two didn't fit on Hypatia's love cot like she'd claimed, Celeste was feeling played out. And all on a few hours of sleep sitting in her kitchen chair. She needed sleep, and she needed a new idea, because the way it was going now wasn't working out.

"Hypatia's resting." Lilitha sidled into the room, eyes cutting briefly to Celeste as she slithered over to the stove.

She made a show of poking at the embers and casting glances her way, until Celeste finally said, "Out with it, then. Say what you came in here to say."

She thrust her pointed chin forward. "She ain't no saint, you know. That sister of yours."

"Never said she was."

"But you worship her like one. Put her up on a pedestal. Always bragging about how pretty she is or that she could sing in the capital. Well, I've been to the capital, and there's plenty of ladies there just as good."

Jealousy. Celeste had seen it from the saloon girls often enough, especially those who had ambitions beyond slinging drinks and talking up strangers for tips. Her guess was Lilitha wanted to be a singer in her own right.

"You got something to say to help me, or you just want to run your jaw?"

Lilitha stiffened, offended. "Hypatia told me all about you. How you think you're better than us 'cause you don't got no Mark. Growing up all hoity-toity among the Elects. Getting educated. But I don't see nothing special about you or your sister. Common Fallen trash, just like the rest of us."

Oh. Celeste realized the girl wasn't just jealous of Mariel, she was jealous of her. She was going to have a conversation with Hypatia about pillow-talking with her belles.

"I was born right here in the Drench," Celeste said plainly, and just as she had shifted her speech when talking to Ibrahim, she could feel herself falling into the cadences of the Drench. Which was the truer version of herself she didn't know, despite what Hypatia insisted. Perhaps both, perhaps neither. "I lived down south with my pa for a while, but it was no society affair, like you think it was. He was a hard man and absent most of the time. And when he died, I was left penniless and practically run out of town on account of his business partner knowing I was Fallen."

Lilitha eyed her suspiciously, as if trying to decide what to make of Celeste's confession. She leaned back, arms folded across her middle. "You're not the only one with education. I used to be a healer. Even apprenticed with a real nurse for it."

"Doing what? Sweeping floors and filling water bottles?"

Folk healing was big business, but most nurses did domestic work, not medicine. Even so, nurses did have access to medicines, and since most Fallen couldn't afford doctors, common ailments were treated with a tonic or the right mix of herbs. Having access to a nurse would have meant something, but Celeste was not feeling generous.

"And if you know healing, what are you doing as a saloon girl?"

Lilitha's chin dipped down to her chest. "Had a bad batch of restoratives, and some people died. Wasn't my fault, but they blamed me. People stopped coming around." She looked up, defiant. "But I got a new line coming out. No thanks to that sister of yours."

"I don't see what Mariel has to do with—"

"She tried to keep that doctor of hers from talking to me. Jealous is what she was, even though she knows I'm with Hypatia. It's not my fault if he had a wandering eye."

Celeste frowned. "What doctor?"

"Lili." That was Hypatia, who'd come to the doorway. She threw a warning glance at her girl.

"What doctor?" Celeste asked again, willing to take an answer from either of them. "Was Mariel sick? Why didn't she say anything? If she's ill, that cave of a jail cell will only make it—"

"She's not ill, Celeste." Hypatia cut her off.

"Oh, but she was getting a thorough physical examination," Lilitha said, cackling.

Hypatia frowned. "Out."

The girl looked like she wouldn't budge, but Hypatia said, "Please," and that dislodged her. She left, rolling her hips and making a show of it. Hypatia reached over to close the door behind her and then came to sit across from Celeste at the table.

"Mariel was stepping out with a doctor."

"Impossible," Celeste scoffed. "I would have known. She would have told me."

"She didn't want to tell you because he's Elect, and she thought you wouldn't understand. What with you hating your father and all."

"She was right!" Celeste rubbed at her neck. "What was she thinking? She knows the Elect can't be trusted."

"See, that's what I mean. She didn't want to hear you on it, because she knows you can't see yourself clear around the subject."

"See myself clear? I know how they think, Hyp. I grew up with them. I hear what they say about us, about Fallen women, when no one but their own kind is there to listen. Whores, mawks.

Insatiable like animals. Good enough to stick your prick in, but don't bring her home."

"All right, all right." Hypatia waved her down. "I know there's a lot of scoundrels out there, but her Daniel seemed different."

"Wait, you've met him?" That stung. "Why didn't you tell me?" Her eyes widened. "Was he there last night?"

"I already told you why I didn't tell you, and no, he wasn't there. Of course, with all the costumes…" She shook her head. "No, I woulda noticed."

"This was happening in the Eden? Behind my back?"

"Not behind your back. Well, not at first. He'd come to one of her performances a few months back. I think it was that time you stayed home with the croup. And they hit it off. It was respectable, and he's charming."

"They always are," she muttered.

"And I started lending her my office for a little privacy."

"I'm surprised you didn't buy her a white gown and set her up at the Velvet Pearl. Charge a dollar for a look-see."

Hypatia's eyes got big, and she snapped her mouth shut.

Celeste didn't care. She knew Hypatia wasn't prostituting her sister out, but this was just as bad. Maybe worse. At least, if she was the sporting type, she'd be getting paid. "He's going to break her heart."

"You're not real clear on matters of the heart, either, Celeste."

"Don't use what happened between me and Abraxas as an excuse for keeping things from me."

Hypatia shrugged, unrepentant. "Mariel knows what she's doing. She's not the shrinking violet you think she is."

Celeste had nothing to say to that. She knew her sister wasn't weak, but she was delicate. An artist and a beauty, who'd had a hard childhood and was no doubt susceptible to a smooth-tongued man.

"I've got to go." She stood up.

Hypatia rubbed a tired hand over her face. "Don't leave here mad, Cece."

"No one calls me Cece but my family," she said, tone icy and distant as Abaddon's peaks.

Hypatia reared back like she'd slapped her, and Celeste guessed she had. But she'd hurt her first, she reasoned, and worse.

Celeste left, walking past Lilitha, who was lounging on the settee pretending to read the paper. The saloon girl gave her a nasty smirk on her way out, but Celeste ignored it. Lilitha was nothing to her. But Hypatia? Her betrayal was a punch in the gut.

She made it back to the boardinghouse in a daze. Mrs. Ruth called out from the dining room, where she'd left out a late supper. Celeste called back something about not feeling well.

Once in her room, she stripped off her clothes and fell into bed. The bed she usually shared with her sister. Mariel's spot was cold and empty. Celeste ran a hand across the sheets.

"I would have understood," she whispered. "You could have told me."

Mariel wasn't there to answer, and she might never be if Celeste couldn't find out what had truly happened in that room last night. She couldn't understand why Mariel would lie to her about the laudanum and the bed... unless she was protecting someone.

Celeste rolled over onto her back to stare at the ceiling. That had to be it. Whoever this Daniel was, Mariel must be lying to protect him. It would be just like an Elect to drag Mariel into some mess and expect her to cover for his nefarious dealings.

Her gaze fell to the window. It was locked tight, the curtains pulled against the night. During their affair, the open window had been a sign to Abraxas that she wanted to see him, that he was welcome. She thought about opening it now. She wanted to ask what he thought of this new revelation, whom he thought Mariel might be protecting.

But she couldn't. She had been lucky to leave their last encounter with her soul and her dignity intact. She didn't dare risk seeing him again, no matter how alone she felt.

She turned her back to the window and forced herself to sleep.

CHAPTER 10

CELESTE DREAMED OF dancing. She had never been very good despite the hours of lessons her father had forced upon her, hoping to pass her off in Elect society. But in her dream, she was as graceful as any proper lady. Her partner led her onto a polished floor of black obsidian. They were alone, the shadowy space lit only by small blue flames flickering atop black wax candles. She wore a dress of red satin, the neckline low, the back sheer, and her arms bared. Waves of fabric billowed behind her as the man who held her drew her close. She could not see his face, only feel his strong hand at her waist, his rough cheek against hers. Her nose grazed the curve of his neck, and she smelled rosewood and amber.

The music began, a sensual duet of fiddle and guitar. They moved—languid, patient—as they found their rhythm. His lead was subtle, the pressure of fingers against skin, the touch of hips as they turned, their bodies molded into one.

"It could be like this forever, Celeste," he whispered, his voice the brush of silk against her skin. "All you have to do is say yes."

She opened her mouth to answer—

And bolted awake, a cry in her throat and sweat hot on her neck. She grasped at the sheets, expecting red satin, before she recognized the familiar bed, the well-worn room. She threw the bedding off and stumbled to the washbasin. She splashed cold water on her face and neck and waited for her heartbeat to cool.

In the mirror, she saw Abraxas's pendant still resting against the hollow between her breasts. Furious at his invasion, she thought to rip the pendant off but instead found herself studying the reflection of it in the mirror, her fingers wound in the cord. She had not had time to learn anything of the sigils etched in the pendant, and even now she did not recognize them, but she wondered if there was something there that allowed the demon lord into her dreams.

Dreams that left her sweating in her bed, dreams where she willingly promised her soul to him. Almost.

"He wouldn't," she whispered, but of course he would. And at every chance. She looked to the window, convinced she would find it open, but it remained firmly shut, just as it had been when she went to sleep.

Saints and sinners, she was foolish to let him back into her life. No, not foolish, she reminded herself. Just terribly, terribly desperate.

After that, she dared not sleep again. She dressed quickly and was putting the final pins in her hair when a knock came at her door. Her first thought was of Abraxas, but he was not one to knock, and besides, he preferred the window. She approached cautiously, her mind conjuring Virtues with iron shackles, but she could not imagine them knocking, either.

"Jumping at nothing at all," she chided herself. The knock came again, more urgent this time.

"Who's there?" she called out.

"Open this door, Miss Semyaza. We need to talk."

It was her landlady, Mrs. Ruth.

Celeste opened the door, and without preamble, Ruth extended a hand, the morning paper in it. She peered at the headline and flushed. Here was her opening bid, the cards she had dealt on her visit to Grace at the *Howler*.

"Well." Ruth shook the paper at her. "Take it!"

Daily in hand, Celeste walked to the table, Ruth on her heels. Celeste took a deep breath and braced herself before flattening the paper across the table and reading.

Goetia's Favorite Songbird Kept in Deplorable Conditions! Did the Virtues Arrest the Wrong Woman?

Celeste quickly skimmed the article, and there it was as she had relayed it to Grace, or at least the more sensational parts. The dark cell, the lack of food and water, the bruises on Mariel's face.

She flashed Ruth a half smile, which she did not return. Celeste did not care. It was good. Anything to draw the Virtues out of the shadows where they operated with near impunity, and all the better if Grace's headlines could turn public opinion in favor of Mariel.

"Miss Semyaza." Ruth's sharp tone drew her attention. Now she could see her landlady was furious. "One thing I ask of you, the only thing I ask of you and your sister"—and the way she said "sister" was a warning that Celeste was not going to like what came after—"is to keep this house out of the papers."

Celeste perused the article again. She had asked Grace not to mention the boardinghouse, and the reporter had agreed. Had she decided to do it anyway? "I don't see a mention of the Elysium House."

"It says Mariel Semyaza's name right there." She stabbed a finger at the offending sentence.

"Come now, Mrs. Ruth, it is unlikely that people will see her name and think of the Elysium House."

"Easy enough to look her up in the public records. Why, I've already had a reporter from the *Herald* and two curious citizens stop in this morning alone."

The reporter she could understand, but the others? "Whatever for?"

"To gawk, mostly. One asked to see the murderess's rooms. And offered me a fair sum of money for it, too."

Celeste was horrified. "What did you do?"

"Sent him on his way, of course."

How disconcerting, to know that strangers thought your pain a spectator sport. But perhaps she should have expected it.

"Mrs. Ruth," Celeste said, herself shaken now, "surely you can't blame Mariel for this."

"It may not be her fault, but it is now a problem for all of us. I can't have you bringing attention here. There are too many vulnerable souls under this roof. I don't need the Virtues poking around."

Celeste thought of the single woman three doors down who wrote sensation stories for a newspaper back East and the two women on the second floor whom Mariel once caught canoodling on the stairs. Rumor had it that Mrs. Ruth herself had been a sporting woman for a brief stint in the capital once upon a time.

There were so few places for women like the ones in this house to live as they wished and feel safe. It could be disastrous for the Virtues to start looking too closely at the Elysium residents.

Celeste did not regret going to the paper. She had to do everything she could to save Mariel. But she would not forgive herself if harm came to these women due to her actions.

"You are right, Mrs. Ruth. What can I do to make amends?"

Perhaps it was her humble tone, but Ruth softened. "I am afraid it is too late for amends. And I am truly sorry, Celeste, but I simply cannot have you and Mariel here anymore."

"But the trial is tomorrow, and Mariel is sure to be found innocent."

"It doesn't matter." The landlady drew a sealed letter from her pocket. The insignia of the Order of Chamuel was pressed into the red wax.

Celeste's heart sank. The Virtues had already taken notice. No wonder Ruth wanted her gone.

"You have until end of day tomorrow."

Mrs. Ruth did not linger after that.

Celeste leaned against the door, overwhelmed before the day had begun. So she was to be homeless. It would not be the first time, she thought, remembering the aftermath of her father's death and her subsequent eviction, but the timing could not be worse. The Eden was closed until further notice, which meant she was out of gainful employment, and she may not have burned her bridge with Hypatia, but she'd certainly set it on fire. Before Lilitha, all would have been quickly forgiven, but now she was not sure. No, she would have to find them lodging somewhere else.

She ran through the list of people she might impose on in Goetia. It was depressingly short. There was Abraxas, who she was sure would welcome her into his home and his bed, but that would be lying down with a devil, quite literally, and if she did it, she would not get up the same person. There was Zeke, who might welcome her and Mariel in as friends under such dire circumstances. He lived in the barn out behind the Eden, which served as his home and his workshop. Surely there was room for a temporary cot until she found Mariel and herself new lodging. It was not ideal, but nothing was right now. Zeke's barn would have to do. She decided to call on him first thing.

She still held the letter in her hand, and she tore it open, ripping through the wax seal with her fingernail. It was from Ibrahim.

> *Miss Semyaza,*
> *After our meeting yesterday, I thought we had an understanding. Imagine my disappointment when I woke up and found our business paraded for spectacle upon the front page of Goetia's most salacious rag.*

"Most salacious rag," she murmured, thinking she had chosen right in going to Grace.

> *Your loose tongue has drawn unfortunate attention to me, and the other heads of the Orders, particularly the Order of Azrael, are not amused. As you know, Chamuel is a gentle Order; however, I cannot speak for my brethren...*

She understood a threat when she saw it and quickly read to the end. The letter concluded with a demand to present herself at his office within the hour, a laughable request, as he'd only given her today to clear Mariel's name. She would not waste one precious minute being berated by him.

She stuffed the letter into her pocket and finished getting ready. The back door of the boardinghouse dumped her into an alley. She stayed to the back ways, avoided Elysium Street altogether, until she crossed Tartarus Street. She stayed on Tartarus until she could come down Perdition from the north. The hour was still early to call upon someone unexpectedly, but she found Zeke sitting on a crate in the alleyway between the still-shuttered Eden and the barn he called home and laboratory, a cup of coffee in his hand, the *Howler* on his knee, and a jaunty tune tripping from his lips. He looked up as she approached, and a smile spread like sunlight across his face.

"Celeste!"

"Zeke." She returned his smile. "How are you?"

His face sobered. "I saw the paper, so the real question is, how are you?" He lifted the *Howler*. "It's terrible what they say here. You're going to get Mariel out, aren't you?"

"Yes," she said firmly, as much for herself as for him.

"Good." He looked around, sheepish. "Where are my manners? Can I offer you some coffee? Tea?"

"I'm fine." Her eyes strayed to the barn behind him, the door slightly ajar.

He noticed, and his grin deepened. "Would you like to see inside?"

She had always been curious about Zeke's inventions. He often talked about them on quiet afternoons at the Eden but had been cagey about allowing people into his laboratory to see. It was quite unexpected that he would ask her in now, but she suspected it had something to do with trying to cheer her up.

"I would be honored."

He got to his feet and threw open the barn doors with a flourish. "Welcome to my imaginarium!"

She stepped inside, not sure what to expect. Before her, hidden away in a nondescript one-horse barn off a Perdition Street back alley, was what could only be called a wonderland. All around her, she saw gears and wires and levered machines, all powered by chips of divinity, executed at a level of complexity and skill that she thought only possible to find at the Divinity Expo, where the great minds of the age displayed their inventions. But here was this Fallen boy, no older than twenty-one and a bartender in a saloon, who rivaled their genius.

"Why, Ezekiel Zagan. It's marvelous."

He beamed. "I've been collecting the divinity for years now, just scrap mostly from the wash, but it's enough to power my machinery. If I could get my hands on enough, I think, well, I think I could make just about anything!"

"I have no doubt." She looked around in wonder, her eye catching on a pair of ladies' earrings lying on a table. Sunflowers dangling from small hoops, shaped from silver, their centers golden divinity.

"It's a hearing device," he explained, picking up one of the metal flowers. "It amplifies sound when you wear it next to your ear."

"And what's this?" she asked, pointing at a contraption made of winding coils and levers.

"This?" He reached out to turn a wheel on the machine, releasing a steady blast of steam. "This is my coffee maker."

She laughed at her mistake, and he flushed, clearly abashed.

"Oh, but here…" He threaded his way through the cramped space to the center of the room. "This is my masterpiece."

He removed a tarp with a showman's flourish to reveal a cross between a buggy and a bicycle. It took up most of the space in the center of the small barn.

"I call it the mountain trike," he explained. "It has three wheels, nubbed and spoked for rough terrain. The frame is slung low for balance, and here"—he opened a door in the heart of the contraption—"is the engine."

She leaned over to look inside and spied the telltale glow of divinity.

"You still have to crank it up, here." He closed the door and fit a small hand crank into a gear. "But once the initial spark is ignited, the divinity does the real work."

"It is a wonder," she said appreciatively. "As good as anything at the exhibit hall on Aventum."

He pressed his hand over his heart, obviously pleased at her praise. "But you didn't come to see my contraptions," he said, face sobering.

"No," she admitted. "I have a favor to ask."

"Name it."

"Mariel and I have been evicted."

A frown marred his bright features, and he opened his mouth, no doubt ready to protest on her behalf, but she waved him down.

"No, it's fine. Really. I understand my landlady's reasoning, and she's not wrong. Besides, it might be better for us to be somewhere else for a while." She told him of the strangers who had come offering bribes for a glimpse into their lives.

His face darkened even more. "Let them try that here, and they'll run up against a pill."

"So we can stay?"

And now his anger turned to concern. "I'd say yes in a minute, you know I would. But Hypatia owns the barn. You'll have to ask her."

Of course. Celeste had forgotten all about that. "No," she said flatly.

"I'm sure she'll say yes."

"No, she won't."

Zeke eyed her suspiciously. "Did you two have a falling-out?"

"Something like that." Celeste sighed, her hopes of an easy solution dashed. "Never mind, then, Zeke. I'll find somewhere else."

"A hotel perhaps?"

"With what money?" She had a little saved but couldn't imagine any hotel in Goetia allowing Mariel in, so obviously Fallen and recently accused of murder.

Zeke rubbed at his ear, thinking. "There are families in the Drench that take on boarders sometimes for trade or whatnot," he said. "Perhaps you can look there."

"I'll try it," Celeste said brightly, not meaning it but saying it for his sake.

"Or you could just talk to Hypatia," he offered, sheepish.

She shook her head. "She'll want me to apologize."

His big eyes got bigger. "What'd you do?"

"It's between her and me," she said, stubborn. "She knows."

"You're gonna have to talk to her sometime," he said, "once the Eden reopens."

"And I will. Then. But not now. Now I've got to save Mariel."

CHAPTER 11

CELESTE'S FIRST STOP after leaving Zeke was the *Howler*. She wanted to congratulate Grace on a successful front page and let her know that the Virtues had threatened the residents of the boardinghouse. Not directly, maybe, but if something were to happen, she wanted Grace to know. The two women were not quite friends, but Grace had believed her and had in a way become her partner in Mariel's defense. The *Howler* had been game to print her news despite knowing it might put them at odds with the Virtues.

"I'll risk it," Grace had assured her yesterday. "There is freedom of the press in Goetia, last I checked, and I dare the Virtues to say otherwise. Besides, the readers will love your story."

Celeste now approached the offices of the *Howler*, hopeful. There was a sign hanging from the door that warned that all copies of the daily were sold out, and she took that as a good sign, but when she opened the door, she found only the editor, a man named Song whom Grace had introduced her to briefly the day before, bent over the typesetter.

"She's not here," he said, recognizing Celeste. "And she won't be back."

"Until tomorrow?"

"Until forever," he growled. "She's sacked. Goddamned Virtues came by and confiscated all the extra papers. Took 'em and weren't even gonna pay until I pitched a fit."

"But it says they're sold out."

"Sure, well, what was I supposed to say?"

"And my landlady had one. And another friend."

"First editions made it out, but I was ready to print more before them Whites showed up."

Celeste's heart thumped in her chest. "And Grace?"

"They were itching to arrest her for sedition, if you can believe it, so I distracted them while she slipped out the back."

Saints and sinners, they'd almost arrested Grace? "Do you know where she is?"

Song eyed her, as if deciding whether she was to be trusted with the information.

"You're right not to tell me," Celeste said. "I'm the one who got her into this mess."

"It was a good story," he protested. "Best thing we've run in ages."

"It wasn't worth it if her life is in danger and her livelihood threatened."

The man grunted at that and seemed to make up his mind. "She's got a mother an hour south of here. I reckon that's where she ran." He pushed ink-stained hands through his dark hair. "I never thought I'd see it," he said, more to himself than to Celeste. "Virtues harassing decent people."

Celeste thought to point out that the Virtues had been harassing Fallen for as long as she could remember, and weren't they decent people? But Song had a point. The daily paper had been confiscated, and Grace had been run out of her job. Celeste had underestimated what the Virtues were willing to do to an Elect woman, and now Ibrahim's invitation sat heavy in her pocket.

She left the *Howler*, glancing down the street as she stepped off the porch. She caught a glimpse of a man turning the corner. Had he been watching her? Had he followed her from the Eden? She had been careless, not imagining the Virtues would go so far, lulled to safety by Ibrahim and her position as *advocatus*. A position she thought would protect her, but that was when she was presumed docile. Going to the paper had proved her otherwise, and now everything held an air of menace. She cursed herself for her carelessness, but the damage had been done.

The women at the boardinghouse, Zeke and Hypatia at the Eden, Grace. They were all in danger because of her. The only person she wasn't worried about was Abraxas. She doubted even the Virtues would dare to cross the demon lord directly.

She ducked around the corner and through the alley, taking turns at random, squeezing through narrow passes between buildings and surprising stable hands, until she found herself on Main Street, not far from the courthouse. The Hall of Records wasn't much farther, and Mrs. Ruth had given her an idea. If the Hall of Records allowed strangers to find out where Mariel lived, then it should allow her to do the same for others. And Lilitha had unwittingly given her a lead to follow: Dr. Daniel.

The Hall of Records was a nondescript building possessing none of the grandeur of other municipal buildings in town. No statues of archangels or founding fathers, no towering columns or divinity-dusted cement. Just a brick building with a slanted roof.

Inside was a businesslike lobby with two large wooden tables, chairs, and three clerk's windows. At each window was a Taborite, gold and glowing with divinity, their engines humming low and steady.

One turned its faceless head to her as she approached. She had never spoken to an automaton before and wasn't sure how they worked. She saw no ears, no mouth. But it seemed to be waiting, expectant.

"I'd like to see the town registry," she said, leaning forward and raising her voice.

She did not know if it understood her at first, but presently it wheeled away to the shelves of archives behind it and after a moment returned with three oversized bound volumes from a shelf. It extended a clawlike hand through the window opening, and she took the ledgers.

"Thank you," she said, feeling a bit foolish. She did not know if Taborites cared to be thanked for their labor, but it seemed the right thing to do.

She took the registers to a vacant table and got to work. Her pencil in hand, she spread her notebook before her and opened the earliest record. If Daniel was a doctor, he was no doubt in the town registry. All she had to do was find him.

It took her an hour to make her way through the first ledger. She collected twenty men over the age of eighteen named Daniel, but only two had professions relevant to medicine. One was a veterinarian, and the other specialized in ancient medicines.

In the next book, there were more Daniels, but most overlapped from the previous year, and none of the new Daniels listed his profession as a medical man.

In the last book, she netted two new Daniels, one a dentist and one a surgeon.

Four Daniels who could be considered doctors, and she had their last names and street addresses. It was a solid place to begin.

She returned the ledgers to the automaton clerk with another thank-you and headed back out into the day, this time making sure to watch her back.

Her first two inquiries were unsuccessful. One was at a boardinghouse where the surgeon Daniel had once resided, but he had moved on sometime last year. The second Daniel was alive but a bedridden gentleman of at least seventy-five. On the third try, she struck gold.

The house of Daniel Alameda was a Victorian on Gethsemane Street only a short stroll off Main. A stone wall with metal fencing encircled the home, but the gate was unlocked, so Celeste let herself in. The facade of the house was imposing, red brick and black trim, and there, above the lintel, so small you would not notice it if you were not looking for such a thing, was a rod of healing that marked the resident as a member of the Order of Raphael.

She knocked, and as she waited for someone to answer, her mind snagged on the rod of healing above the door. The rod proved the resident of the home was a Virtue, and the name and profession from the records confirmed a Daniel lived here who was a doctor. There was something about the Order of Raphael, something she was forgetting. Was it Mr. Ibrahim or Abraxas who had mentioned it? Or maybe Lilitha. She could not remember.

Before she could sort the memory out, the door creaked open. The woman before her was tall and candlewick-thin, her narrow face sunken. Her skin was white. Not the cheerful ruddy-cheeked white of Mr. Ibrahim but the colorless white of bones bleached by the sun. Her dress was black and a decade out of fashion, buttoned tight to her wrinkled neck.

"May I help you?" the woman asked, her voice warm as midwinter frost.

"I'm looking for Daniel Alameda."

"And who are you?"

Celeste thought it best to lie. Explaining she was there on behalf of her sister who was possibly having a steamy affair with the man seemed unwise. "Daniel was helping me with a medical issue. Is he in?"

The woman's unwelcoming facade slipped for a moment, and Celeste saw there was grief behind it, but she quickly recovered her cold demeanor. "Daniel's dead. And frankly, you've got a lot of nerve coming here."

She started to close the door.

"Wait!" Celeste moved to hold the door open.

The woman stopped, long enough to look down her nose at Celeste in disgust.

"I'm so sorry, but did you say... dead? Dr. Daniel is deceased?" And the dread that had been building all morning as the bad news piled up reached a deafening crescendo in her head.

The woman's voice was caustic with scorn. "Did I speak too slowly? Too quickly? In a language you don't understand?"

"No, of course not, Mrs. Alameda," Celeste said hurriedly, realizing the woman must be Daniel's wife, because of course he had a wife. *Oh, Mariel*, she thought, *you foolish, foolish girl*. "It's just quite the shock."

"Perhaps the greater shock to the likes of you is that Daniel had a wife at all."

The likes of you. It seemed Mariel was not the only time her husband had strayed.

"I think there's a misunderstanding—" Celeste began.

"Girls like you are nothing," Mrs. Alameda spat. "A foul habit that I tolerated because he always came back to me. To me!" And now her veneer cracked completely, a sob racking her body, her shoulders heaving. "But now one of you little monsters have taken him from me for good. To hell with you, all of you! May the devil take your soul!" She lunged at Celeste, her fingers extended like claws.

Celeste threw herself back, tripping down the porch stairs. She cried out, arms seeking purchase, but caught only air. She landed hard on her back, the breath flying from her lungs.

Mrs. Alameda stood on the steps over her, glaring down, and for a moment, Celeste thought she might come for her. She shuffled away, crablike, putting distance between her and the grief-stricken woman.

Mrs. Alameda's glare morphed into triumph as she looked down at Celeste, fallen in the dirt and ash. It seemed enough to satisfy her, and she retreated into the house, slamming the door behind her.

Celeste groaned in pain, her heart still racing. Then she remembered that a woman like Mrs. Alameda might well have a shotgun, and something told Celeste the woman wouldn't hesitate to use it. She scrambled to her feet, picked up her skirts, and ran. She didn't care who saw her. She only wanted to be as far away as possible from this cursed house and its bitter inhabitant.

CHAPTER 12

ONCE CELESTE WAS well down Gethsemane and the Alameda house was no longer in view, she stopped to catch her breath. Despite the awful encounter, she had learned valuable information. Mariel's Daniel was dead, and he had been a Virtue. It was not a distant leap to assume he was the murder victim, although she would have to confirm it with Ibrahim. And now she remembered who had told her of the Order of Raphael. It had been Grace, speaking of the victim and calling him a saint.

"A saint who couldn't keep his trousers up," Celeste observed to no one.

His widow had certainly implied that Daniel had multiple mistresses, which meant Mariel was possibly only one of many. Which also meant any number of women might have castrated Dr. Daniel. Hell, his wife alone seemed perfectly capable of the deed, although her misery had seemed genuine.

Perhaps another woman had framed up Mariel well and good. But who? It would have to be someone who had earned her trust. Someone who might encourage her to share a bottle of laudanum. It seemed outrageous. It was much more likely that Daniel's murder was the result of some business dealing gone wrong, and Mariel had simply gotten caught up in it.

"Excuse me, Miss."

A young blond man was leaning patiently against the iron gate a few paces away, waiting for Celeste to notice him. He was handsome and well groomed and carried himself with the air of a moderately successful man assured of his future wealth. Nothing about the man before her shouted Virtue, and perhaps at another time she would not have been attuned to such a thing. But she needed only to glance at the small scales pinned to his lapel to know he was a member of the Order of Chamuel. And she was sure he was the man she had seen turn the corner outside the *Howler*.

"Are you the one who's been following me?" she asked, but she already knew. She was keenly aware of the dagger against her wrist.

"You received a letter at the Elysium House for Single Women?" He did not wait for her reply but continued, "Then you know why I am here."

"I asked if you have been following me."

His smile was thin. "We have eyes and ears everywhere, Miss."

Of course they did, and of course a pair of them would be sent to bring her to Mr. Ibrahim, whether she liked it or not.

"Are you the one who threatened Grace?"

He stared blankly at her. "Who is Grace?"

"From the *Howler*."

He still feigned ignorance, and she could feel her temper rising.

"And if I refuse to go with you?"

His thin smile stretched to nothing. "I'm afraid I cannot allow that."

"Of course you can't." There was no avoiding Ibrahim, and now she was not sure she wanted to. This lackey might act ignorant, but Ibrahim wouldn't dare. "Lead the way."

She expected to return to the territorial court and the office at the end of the elevator with the hearth and the bookshelves, but instead they walked down Main. She caught a glimpse of herself and the Virtue in the pharmacy window. How normal they looked. An attractive if slightly harried young woman and a handsome man as her companion. Hypatia had urged her to pursue this life. Acceptance, respectability, the comfort of conformity, and the security that came with it. She could almost hear the bar owner's voice: *All this striving, all this rebelling, and for what?* When she could pass into Elect society and pretend that Abraxas and Hypatia and all the rest—Zeke, the Eden, the boardinghouse—had never happened.

But she could not forget Mariel, and for a moment, she hated her sister for it.

She shoved the thought away, wretched and ashamed.

And then the reflection in the window was changing, the blond man's long locks becoming short and black, his day suit midnight brocade, his pale skin rich ink. She quickly turned away, unwilling to face Abraxas's mocking smile, which she was sure would be looking back at her from the reflected glass.

You would forget me? he asked. *Abandon me in favor of mediocrity? Respectability?*

"Leave me alone!" she shouted.

"Are you all right?" the Elect man asked.

She looked at him, shocked, and then at the reflection. Herself, the man, and no Abraxas.

"I'm sorry, I..." What could she say when he was looking at her like that? She settled for "I'm fine," and gestured for him to lead on.

Soon enough, they arrived at their destination. The Excelsior Hotel was the finest hotel in town and perhaps the finest building, too. Unlike the Eden, the structure had not been made with divinity cement but rather with white marble. Six massive Doric columns ran across the front of the building, as imposing and perfect as a Grecian temple, and a small pediment graced the front entrance, with a larger one along the rooftop in replica that bore the hotel's name. Inside, the floors were marble and the walls rare pink ivory, all imported from places far away and impossible to reach without the aid of divinity-driven technology. It was a cathedral built to worship the wealth that flowed from the mine and the wealthy men who claimed it as their own.

They entered through the main door and turned right into the dining room. The cream of Goetia's Elect society was gathered for luncheon: mine owners, judges, politicians. There at a table in the far corner sat Ibrahim. He wore a fine suit, and his silver hair was oiled and trimmed. He looked the part of a distinguished town father, and she wondered what his profession was. In the excitement of yesterday's meeting, she had failed to ask.

The Virtue who had led her this far pointed to a seat across from Ibrahim. She sat, her back to the room, and folded her hands in her lap. The Virtue pulled a privacy curtain closed before joining them at the table. The curtain would keep out casual prying eyes, and if someone were to catch a glimpse, they would only see a young woman and her male companion seated across from Mr. Ibrahim, no doubt his guests for lunch.

Ibrahim was already well into his meal. His plate consisted of a bloody bit of red meat accompanied by fried eggs, potatoes, and, at his elbow, a bowl-sized cup of coffee. He spoke without looking up from his plate, his knife, fork, and mouth working without rest.

"Would you care to join me for luncheon, Miss Anant?"

"It's Anant today?" she asked, feeling sour and still smarting from her revelation about her own hypocrisy.

"We're in mixed company. Surely you understand the delicate nature of our acquaintance."

She glanced over at the Virtue next to her. He had walked with her through the street, made small talk of a sort. If he knew she was Fallen, would he have spoken to her so civilly? Or would he have dragged her to Ibrahim in chains instead?

Ibrahim grunted, as if reading her mind and acknowledging the truth of her conclusion.

"I received your summons." She took the letter from her pocket and held it up. Another paper came with it, the handbill from Hypatia's office, the one offering quick money for the sale of homes in the Drench. She stuffed it back into her coat.

"I believe I asked you to come within the hour, which would have been…" He paused only long enough to check his timepiece. "Six hours ago."

"I was delayed. I am in the middle of an investigation, as you might know."

He smiled, as if she had amused him, but his delight passed quickly, and his face fell to sterner lines. "We must talk about your relationship to the *Daily Howler*."

"Yes, we must. Some of your brethren harassed the editor and threatened to arrest my friend."

He paused, fork halfway to his mouth. "That is no one's fault but your own. What did you expect to happen?"

"I expected the daily newspaper to be—"

"Untouchable?" His tone was mocking. "Respected? You overplayed your hand, and while I admire the effort, there are consequences."

"I understand you are vexed—"

"Vexed?" He slammed down his utensils. "I am beyond

vexed. I don't think you understand the gravity of what you have done. The Order has been at my neck, inquiring as to who you are and what merits you possess that warrant your assignment as *advocatus diaboli*."

"Can they do that? Remove me?"

"No, it is my decision alone. But they can make me regret it." He sighed. "They wished to know your relationship to the accused."

"Did you tell them I am her sister?"

He glanced at the blond Virtue. Celeste could feel the man's eyes upon her but ignored him. She did not care to keep the secret of her heritage, even if Ibrahim did. Even if she knew it put her at further risk among these people and in this place. She refused to be ruled by her basest desires.

"Mr. Ibrahim." She calmly ignored the waves of censure drifting off the man next to her. "Do you wish to remove me as *advocatus*?" She asked it coolly, but her heart was thudding in her chest.

"Can you promise me you will stay away from the press?"

"Will you leave Grace alone?"

"After the trial, she does not concern us, assuming you stay away." His gaze was fixed on her, refusing to let her go until she gave an answer.

She hated to concede, but for Grace's sake, she did. "If you give me no reason to speak further to the *Howler*, then I shall not."

"That is all I ask," he said, magnanimous, before resuming his lunch. He gestured at her with his knife, continuing on as if nothing had happened. "You will be happy to know that I've had the accused moved to a place that should meet with your approval. Fresh clothing, meals, medical care." He sawed at a tendon in his steak. "Light."

"Is my sister free to return home?" she asked stiffly.

"Of course not."

"Then it does not meet with my approval."

He grunted, as if she was ungrateful. No doubt he thought she should praise him. But he had only provided Mariel with the basics of human decency after Grace's article had pressured him into it.

"I would ask something else of you," Celeste said, feeling as if she had nothing to lose. "I want to know more about Daniel Alameda."

Ibrahim sipped from his coffee, no doubt buying time. His gaze turned to the Virtue, who was staring at Celeste, still radiating sour outrage.

"You. Go get Miss Anant coffee," Ibrahim ordered.

The Virtue's mouth turned down in disapproval. "I know what she is, and she's not an 'Anant.'" He hissed the accusation, his eyes seeking out some tell on her skin or in the curl of her hair, since she did not bear the Mark.

"Choose your words carefully," Ibrahim warned. "Remember where you are, and who I am, and that she is under my protection here."

"You had me walk the streets with her, knowing she was a Fallen? What if people saw? What will they think?"

"Is that your concern? You stupid boy." Ibrahim leaned in, and Celeste saw another side of him. He became someone to fear. "I don't give a good goddamn what they think. Now, go get the coffee."

The Virtue puffed his chest, one last stand, but he only sounded petulant. "Make her get her own coffee. I am not a servant, particularly to her kind."

"You are whatever I say you are. Go! Now!"

The Virtue jumped to his feet, finally realizing his immediate danger. He went to duck under the curtain, and Celeste reached out. He froze when her fingers touched the bare skin of his wrist.

"With plenty of sugar, if they have it."

The Virtue's glare cut across her like jagged glass.

"And take the long way back," Ibrahim added.

He went without further protest, cradling his wrist as if she had drawn blood.

"The Excelsior has plenty of sugar, I assure you, Miss Anant," Ibrahim said, as if she'd just asked the sun whether it knew how to shine.

She smiled tightly. "Then he should have no trouble fulfilling my request."

He stared at her a long moment before a low chuckle escaped from his mouth. "I see." Bits of food clung to his beard, and he took up his napkin to wipe them away. "You shouldn't provoke him like that. One day, you'll do it to the wrong man, and he'll kill you for it." He said it matter-of-factly.

She kept the smile on her face despite the sharp terror that tightened her throat. For a moment, she had thought Ibrahim an ally, but his comment was a reminder that no Virtue could be a true ally, only a man with whom she temporarily shared a common enemy.

"Tell me about Virtue Daniel," she said.

Ibrahim's gray eyebrows rose. "So, you have discovered that he was the victim."

"Tell me what you know of him. I've earned that much."

He pushed his plate away, satiated, and focused his attention on her. "What can I say? He was a member of the Order of Raphael. Young. Well favored. But I had only met him once or twice. He was not Chamuel, and we tend to stay with our own Order."

"And his wife?"

Something must have shown in her face, because he asked, "You've met her, then?"

She nodded.

"A shrew of a woman. Much older than he, and wealthy. I gather theirs was not a love match."

She had no affection for Mrs. Alameda, but if she had been married to such a faithless man, she might have earned the title of shrew herself. "I believe she loved him, but that is neither here nor there. What of his business dealings, his social life beyond his marriage?"

She still thought that someone else had been in that room, whether a spurned mistress or a wronged business partner.

Ibrahim frowned. "Daniel Alameda is not on trial."

"Considering the time and place of the murder and its personal nature, I believe the killer and he were acquainted. I want to know whom he associated with in his final days. That's all."

He sat for a moment, studying her. Whatever he saw made him nod sharply. "As you wish, Miss Anant." He reached up to his lapel and unpinned the scales there. He slid the ornament across the table. "He was in business with the head of the Order of Raphael. Whatever Daniel was doing in his last days, he will know. Show him this, use my name, and he will speak to you."

"And who is he?"

Ibrahim motioned toward her pocket. Confused, she pulled the handbill out and gave it to him. He spread it open on the table and pointed to the name at the bottom.

"Mr. Tabor, the owner of the mine?" She was surprised, although she should not have been. He was one of the most powerful men in Goetia. Of course, he was a Virtue and the head of an Order. "Daniel was in the mining business? This handbill was his?"

"Indeed." Ibrahim called for the check.

The Virtue had not returned with her coffee, but Ibrahim did not seem like he planned to wait. He shrugged into his coat with the help of a member of the waitstaff and offered her a farewell.

"Until tomorrow at the trial," he said, a hint of eagerness in his voice. "High noon sharp. Do not be late. For Mariel's sake."

And then he was gone.

She followed his cue and did not wait, either, half-convinced the blond man would show up and put a knife in her back instead. Although she was so tired that she might have suffered it for the boost the coffee and sugar provided.

"No time for such things," she told herself, pushing to her feet. "Mr. Tabor awaits."

CHAPTER 13

EVERYONE KNEW THE Tabor house. It was the grandest home on Ambrosia Street, and Ambrosia Street was the grandest street in Goetia. The Elect called it Rich Man's Row and were certain God favored the men and women who lived within its well-kept palaces. But the Fallen called Ambrosia Street the Eye of the Needle, and they were certain those within would burn in the pits of hell upon their deaths.

The street was only a short distance from the Excelsior Hotel, and she arrived at Tabor's grand manse within the quarter hour. The manservant who greeted her at the door informed her that Mr. Tabor was indisposed and not seeing guests. She showed him Ibrahim's pin. He looked at it, handed it back, and then disappeared into the vast residence. He returned a moment later to give her a slip of paper with an address and a drawing of a map.

"What is this?" she asked.

"Directions to Mr. Tabor's laboratory."

She recognized the general area the map portrayed and the X that marked Tabor's laboratory. It was part of the divinity mine complex that spread across one of the lower peaks known as Abaddon's Hands. It was ten miles up the mountain, too far to walk. There were few hours left in the afternoon, so even if she did find a horse and buggy to take her up to the mine, she suspected no one would want to wait for the nighttime return trip.

"When do you expect him home?" she asked the manservant, hoping she could call again after dinnertime.

"Not until tomorrow."

"Tomorrow?" Every moment, the clock ticked closer to Mariel's trial. She needed to talk to Tabor tonight.

She walked back to the Excelsior and attempted to hail a carriage, but none was willing, citing, as expected, the steep roads and lateness of the hour.

She needed another option, and the idea came to her all at once.

She hurried across town to Perdition. It was that strange hour between day and night, the sky streaked red with the last vestiges of sunlight. The street was beginning to buzz with pleasure-seekers, and the air was redolent with opium. The Eden was still closed, but other establishments had flung their doors open to the night, music and laughter filling the streets.

She turned down the alley, hoping to find Zeke's barn doors open and him on his crate, but they were closed tight, and no light shone from inside. She knocked, but no one answered. She tried the door, and, to her surprise, it pushed open.

"Zeke?" she called into the dark.

He wasn't there, but she couldn't wait.

There, in the center of the room, was the mountain trike he had displayed so proudly. She remembered the drawer where he'd kept the key and retrieved it.

"Zeke?" she called one last time, words of excuse ready

on her tongue should he catch her stealing his most prized possession. But there was only silence.

"I'm sorry," she whispered, hoping perhaps the echo of her regret would linger and soften his anger upon his return, and then she ceased regretting, telling herself this was for Mariel and therefore justified.

She used the key to crank the engine until it hummed, the divinity glowing bright inside, and then steered the thing out of the barn, all the while expecting Zeke to return and catch her red-handed. But he did not, and she was away and down the alley within moments. She stuck to the back ways until she was clear of town so as not to draw too much attention, but people were becoming more accustomed to divinity engines every day. It was only a matter of time before they would be commonplace in Goetia.

The climb was more gradual than she had expected, and she made good time in Zeke's machine. The road was clear, no sign of the donkey-hauled wagons that carried miners from the camp to the mine entrance. It was between shifts, not quite quitting time for the day shift or first bell for the late shift, so she had the road to herself. The trike proved easy to maneuver as it curved around the contours of the mountain, until finally she reached the mine complex.

Tabor's mine was a combination of tall pitched-roof wooden buildings constructed across the valley. The mine entrance itself was somewhere inside it all, a hole and a tunnel that led into the belly of the mountain where Abaddon's body rotted into treasure and birthed man's next great age.

The surrounding structures were the processing plant where rock and divinity were separated. The drainage ran down the peak in man-made rivulets to gather in toxic pools somewhere below. To the west, apart from the main buildings, stood the foreman's house and, of course, Tabor's laboratory.

The lab looked much like Zeke's barn from the outside, only three times its size. Light and noise emanated from within. She left the trike near the wide barn doors and approached, Ibrahim's pin clutched in one gloved hand and the handbill in the other.

The noise was so loud she knew no one inside would hear her shouts, so she went through the unlocked door.

If Zeke's imaginarium was a wonderland, Tabor's laboratory was something more sinister. Here were the same devices, gears and pulleys and engines, but Zeke's creations had been fanciful. Tabor's were not. She spied a revolver, modified with an expanded cylinder that automatically fed more bullets to the gun. There was an automaton like the one in the records hall, but its arms had been replaced with razored disks. And there, on a table, was a cage meant to fit over a human head. Tiny pins jutted inward toward the eyes, and a hinge pried the jaw open. It was a torture device of some kind, she was sure of it.

The deafening noise ended suddenly, and a voice asked, "Who are you?"

She turned to face the speaker. He was of average build and height, although his shoulders rose unusually high on his back, as if he spent much of his time stooped over, and his skin had a sallow, unhealthy cast from spending time indoors. His brown hair was full and unkept, and he looked more mountain man than wealthy mine owner. He wore wire spectacles with thick lenses, and around his neck hung a leather apron that covered his chest and body down to his knees. She noticed his blue eyes had a watery gleam to them, and sweat gathered at his temples and stained his shirtsleeves.

"Are you Virtue Tabor?"

His lips pursed. "Virtue?"

"Virtue Ibrahim sent me," she explained. "Well, I asked him to send me. I was anxious to meet you." She thrust forward her gloved hand, the pin resting on her palm. He peered at her strangely, as if unsure what hands were for, until he noticed the pin. He took it, inspected it closely, and returned it.

"And what does Virtue Ibrahim want?"

"It was me, actually, who wanted something." She dropped the pin into her pocket and produced the handbill for his inspection.

His quick gaze darted across the paper. "You're interested in selling your property?"

"Perhaps."

"Perhaps," he repeated, nodding.

Posing as a potential seller was the best way she had thought of to lower his guard, but she wasn't sure it was working.

He turned away from her and walked back toward the shadowy depths of the laboratory. "You came all the way up Abaddon's Hand at night to speak to me on a perhaps?"

"Yes," she said, hurrying to follow, lest she lose sight of him among the strange mechanicals. "You see, my situation could not wait. I had spoken previously to your partner, a Dr. Daniel, but have been unable to reach him."

"Virtue Daniel is dead," he declared over his shoulder, voice matter-of-fact. "Murdered, from what I understand." He'd stopped at a table with a large magnifier, and she saw he was working on dissecting some kind of mammal. Its fur had been discarded nearby, and its innards glistened wetly under the divinity lamps.

She rubbed her hands across her arms, unsettled. Tabor noticed and chuckled under his breath. "It's science, Miss... ?"

119

"Semyaza." She had thought about what to say, and while Anant afforded her freedom of movement, she didn't feel right using it. It only served to distance her from her Fallen ancestry and from Mariel, and she refused to do that anymore.

"And you say Ibrahim sent you?"

"Yes."

His eyes roved over her form, as if truly noticing her for the first time.

"Tea, Miss Semyaza?" He did not wait for her answer but poured water from a nearby pitcher into a waiting kettle. He turned a knob, and a flame ignited on the burner.

He motioned her toward a wooden stool. She sat, and he positioned himself across from her. "I assume Ibrahim sent you up here to find out why Daniel and I were buying up land in the Drench."

Celeste frowned. "No, I came because—"

"No need to dissemble, Miss Semyaza. I'm happy to tell him. You see, the new lode is ready to be mined, and Ibrahim's too late to stop it. Production begins tomorrow. All I have to do is give the word, and there will be a new vein producing three times as much divinity as Ibrahim's mine." Tabor leaned forward. "I know his mine is drying up, Miss Semyaza. He can't keep that from me." He tapped his temple. "I've got my own spies."

The kettle whistled, and Tabor sprang to his feet. As he prepared the tea, he muttered to himself, words Celeste couldn't quite understand. She suspected the sickness of Abaddon's Revenge had started to pollute his brain. How could it not, when he was surrounded by it here night and day, and in such quantities? His mind was not entirely gone, she did not think, but the paranoia, the gleam to his skin, the madness manifesting in his inventions? The signs were unmistakable.

She was in danger. The realization came all at once. She had to find out what Tabor knew about Daniel's murder and get out as quickly as she could. She turned her wrist, just a fraction. Not enough to release her dagger but enough to assure her that it was there.

She cleared her throat. "Mr. Tabor, I'm afraid you are right, and I haven't been quite honest. I'd like to ask you a few questions about Daniel."

"Tea first," he said brightly, setting a plain but well-made cup before her.

The tea itself was a weak yellowish brew. He stared at her, expectant.

"I'm really not thirsty."

"You think it's poisoned?" He swept up the cup and drank. "Is that better?"

He handed it back, and, thinking to humor him long enough to keep him friendly and ask him her questions, Celeste took a polite sip from the side his lips had not touched.

"Well?"

"It's fine," she allowed, although in fact it was bitter.

"It's a wild variety that grows here on the mountain. It has wonderful medicinal properties." He motioned for her to drink more.

She took one more sip before setting the cup aside. "Now, about Daniel."

He focused on her, his blue eyes sharpening.

"So it's Daniel you care about. And you said it's Semyaza, is it? You're a pretty thing, aren't you? Isn't that why you've truly come?" His tone had shifted to something menacing, quick as lightning.

The back of her neck tingled in alarm, reminding her of the wind that had blown through town on Aventum Angelorum. It would have come down through this very spot, gathering the divinity ash that originated in the processing plants before spreading it down the mountain all the way to Goetia.

"When was the last time you saw him?" she asked.

His eyes narrowed. "It's not Ibrahim at all who's sent you, is it? You've come for the same reason the other girl came."

Unease roiled her stomach. "What other girl?"

"Come now." He *tsk*ed, brows drawing down in disapproval. "We're adults here, are we not? I assume Daniel got into your skirts, too. Whelped a pup or will soon. I told him to convince your kind to sell their land, not cat his way through the lot of you. I refused to pay the other girl he'd gotten in a family way, so don't you expect anything from me." He shook a chiding finger. "This time next year, the town's going to be full of abandons no doubt begging at my door. Well, tell them all that I won't pay, you hear me? Daniel might have been a Virtue and a member of the Order of Raphael, but we owe nothing to his Fallen by-blows, you hear me?"

His words came to her as if from a distance, and her vision blurred. She fell forward, briefly catching herself on the table before her hands slipped and she thudded to the floor, her legs collapsing from beneath.

"Drink, drink." Tabor loomed over her, proffering the teacup. "The tea will make things right."

She tried to push him away, but he forced the cup to her mouth. The bitter brew wet her lips before she gathered the strength to knock his hand away. The cup went flying. She heard it shatter somewhere far away. She tried to climb to her feet and failed. She shook her head violently, trying to clear the haziness, but it was useless.

"Now, now," Tabor said, his hand coming down heavy on her shoulder. "No need to rush. You've just had a spell of some sort. Best to wait it out."

She again tried to stand, but his hand pressed her down. A sliver of panic shot up her spine, momentarily clearing her head. He was staring at her, his eyes distorted through his lenses, waiting.

A sharp pain lanced through her gut, and she bent over, a hiss on her lips.

"Hmm... there, there." He moved away. "I think it's working."

"Wh-what?" She could barely get the word out around the cramps racking her insides.

"I do wish this wasn't necessary. Daniel's murder was a setback, but the plan is almost completed, you see. Because either you're one of Daniel's whores or you're a spy for Ibrahim. Either way, you are a liability."

A spy? But she'd shown him Ibrahim's pin. Surely the Virtue wouldn't have sent her up here to a madman knowing he would suspect her of chicanery. *Oh, fool*, she chided herself. Of course he would. She should have known. He had been too kind, too generous, siding with her over that blond Virtue, doing just enough to gain her trust, making this visit to Tabor seem like her idea.

"Not—" she protested, but that was as far as she managed before she vomited.

She heard Tabor moving around, making clicking noises with his tongue as if unhappy. Her head felt heavy, but she lifted her gaze long enough to meet his eyes.

"Did you... poison me? But you said—!"

"I did nothing of the sort. You only believed I did, but in fact I've built up an immunity to a small quantity of the brew. Foolish girl, not to trust your gut." He paced back and forth. "I'll have to come up with some excuse for your death, or"—his eyes flickered towards the door—"perhaps not. That contraption you came in. Pity you lost control and it went off the side of the mountain. It's a long way down some of these ravines, and the ash is so thick. They won't find your body for weeks, if at all."

Her vision was worsening, and Celeste knew that if she didn't get out of Tabor's laboratory now, she would end up dead at the bottom of a canyon, just as he promised. She forced herself to her feet, knocking over stools and glass bottles as she did. She heard him cry out in alarm, but she kept moving, stumbled toward the exit, her terror acute.

Tabor sighed, trailing behind. "Come now, Miss Semyaza. Is this drama really necessary?"

She flung open the barn door. "Help!" Her voice was barely a whisper. "Someone help me!"

She remembered her dagger, still in the sheath on her forearm. She twisted her wrist, and it came to her hand. When Tabor grabbed her, she turned and swung the little blade with all her might. She heard him shout in pain as she sliced across his stomach. The momentum carried her forward, and she sprawled across the ground, the dagger flying from her spasming fingers.

She heard Tabor yelling, incoherent, his footsteps coming nearer. She crawled on hands and knees, desperately searching for the lost knife. Her hand touched something metallic, but before she could grasp it, Tabor's booted foot came down on her fingers.

She screamed.

He reared back, a kick aimed at her face, a blow that would render her senseless.

She cowered, arms over her head.

The flap of wings roared through her ears, and brimstone filled her nose. Tabor shrieked in terror, and fire filled the night, so hot it burned blue. She caught a glimpse of a sword, black as the hour before dawn, and Tabor's head went flying from his shoulders.

Her stomach turned.

And then Abraxas was there, pulling her into his arms.

"*Tranquilla*," he soothed, his voice like deep water. "You're safe now."

"Poison," she gasped. "He poisoned the tea."

He cursed and sheathed his black blade across his back. He dug a long black fingernail into his palm, a hiss escaping his lips. He gently opened her mouth, and a drop of something that burned like fire touched her tongue. She struggled, afraid, but he soothed her with soft words and rubbed along her jaw and neck until she swallowed.

"Demon blood," he whispered. "It will burn away any contamination."

She wept silently, the shock finally rolling over her.

He stood, her limp form cradled in his arms, her cheek nestled in the curve of his neck. She smelled rosewood and amber, like in her dream.

"Hold on to me, Celeste," he said as they took to the sky.

CHAPTER 14

LATER CELESTE WOULD only remember bits and pieces of their mad flight down the mountain. The tumbling divinity-powered lights of Goetia below her, the bite of the black winds as they flew down Abaddon's Hand, and the heat of Abraxas's blood as it seared her from the inside.

She awoke in an unfamiliar bed, wrapped in thick cotton. A fire blazed in the hearth, and the air smelled rich with spices: cardamom, cinnamon, and clove. She tilted her head and saw that she was in a one-room cabin, spare but tidy. Along the far wall were a cast-iron stove and a white porcelain washbasin and in the middle of the room a kitchen table.

Sitting in a hard chair by the table, looking none too comfortable, was Abraxas. His wings were gone, and his more familiar midnight-blue velvet jacket hung from the back of his chair. He had removed his collar and waistcoat and wore only his shirtsleeves, white linen shirt unfastened at the neck. A book lay open in his hands, the edge of the cover visible.

"Milton?" she asked, her voice scratchy and thin. "There's a nut to crack."

He looked up, face alight, and then his expression cooled

to something more neutral, more careful. "It's all balderdash, anyway." He closed the book, face guarded, and asked, "How are you feeling?"

"I..." She sat up and pressed a hand to her chest. Her skin was hot, as if fevered, but she didn't feel sick. She felt... a hunger. Her eyes fell to Abraxas. His patrician features, his powerful shoulders and arms, the curve of his lush mouth.

"Come here," she said.

His eyes burned crimson, and he almost stood before he stopped himself. "There's something you should know."

She pushed the blanket aside. It was too hot for cotton. Too hot for clothes. She looked down. She was wearing only her linen shift, her arms and legs bare, but even that was too much. She wanted to be naked. She lifted the shift over her head and let it fall to the floor.

She could hear Abraxas catch his breath.

Her smile was a wicked thing. "I said come."

This time, he stood but did not approach her. She could see it took all his willpower to resist, and his gaze did not leave her.

"Why are you fighting me?" she asked, voice rough with desire. She needed to feel the touch of his hands, the hard lines of his body against her own.

He swallowed. "You must understand that I did it to save you."

"If you will not come to me"—she dropped her feet to the floor and stepped forward, arms languid and hips swaying—"I will come to you."

He watched her walk to him, eyes devouring her, and she let him. She felt uninhibited, unafraid. In the moment, she felt truly herself, and she relished it. For once, she was not thinking of Mariel, she was not torn between the Elect and the Fallen. She was at peace, focused on the thing she wanted, and that was the man who stood before her.

She trailed a finger down his chest to his waistband, and then her hand slid lower. He grabbed her wrist before she could find what she wanted, and she moaned in frustration.

"I gave you my blood," he whispered, voice ragged. "To burn out the poison. But it has consequences."

A shiver of awe traced down her back. She knew Abraxas would do nothing that put her life in jeopardy, but her soul was another matter. "Consequences?"

"It is harder to control your desires. This is not you, Celeste. This is… this is me."

She leaned into him so there was no space between them. Her head fit into the hollow of his throat, and she nipped at his neck.

"So, any minute now, I'm going to want to debate theology?" she asked.

He exhaled, laughing roughly.

"This is all me, Abraxas," she assured him. "I can feel the demon blood, but it is giving me clarity, not confusion. I feel focused, like everything else has been a distraction, and I finally understand what I want."

"And what is that?" he breathed.

"You. From the first time I saw you at the Eden, I've wanted you."

He pressed his lips to the top of her head, surprisingly chaste. "Are you sure? Demonkind are not known for their restraint."

She moved quickly, pushing him backward until he hit the wall. This time, her hands found what they wanted. "Then stop resisting."

She bit his lower lip, drawing blood. He roared and took her mouth with his, and her world became a place of heat and desire. Skin and sweat and slick, as he lifted her up and parted her thighs. Pain and pleasure and aching need, as she took him inside her.

Let heaven bear witness, she thought as they moved together. *But let hell judge.*

AFTER, THEY LAY in bed, watching the room lighten with the dawn, the first light of the day creeping in around the edges of the curtains. The effects of the demon blood had waned, but Celeste did not regret what they had done. It had been everything she remembered and more, the pleasure even sweeter since long denied, her abandon more complete under the influence of Abraxas's blood. She closed her eyes, wishing the night would rule for just a little longer.

Abraxas must have sensed her wish, because he curled around her lower body, his mouth tracing the curve of her backbone, leaving a trail of kisses down her spine.

"Stay here with me today," he whispered against her skin.

"Where are we?" She had meant to ask, but other, more pressing issues had taken precedence.

"In the Drench. This is my home."

"The Drench?" she asked, surprised. "What of your house on Ambrosia?" That had been where she had gone to see him before, the place she thought of as his.

"I still own it, but it is not the same with you gone. I prefer here."

She looked around the modest cabin. A single room, spare furniture, the basic necessities, but nothing that suggested the inhabitant was an immortal lord of hell.

"And all your treasures?"

"They will keep. Besides, they are nothing when my greatest treasure is here before me."

She ran a hand through his hair. "I would like nothing more than to stay, but Mariel's trial is at noon."

He stilled. "You still plan to be her *advocatus*?"

"Of course. I gave you my body, Abraxas, not my soul. Mariel still needs me."

She could tell he didn't like that. "And what will you say in her defense?"

She turned to face him, pulling him up so that they were face-to-face. She had been thinking as they lay there, and she had decided. She did not know if he would approve, but it was the best way she could think of to save Mariel.

"I have a plan. Do you know Lilitha?"

He shook his head.

"She's a saloon girl at the Eden, one of Hypatia's passing fancies. She was there Aventum night, and she knew Daniel. She said he made eyes at her, and maybe he did. But she was jealous of Mariel, tried to turn me against her. And she's a healer, knows her way around the human body."

He frowned. "What are you saying?"

"She could have done it."

"But she didn't."

"You don't know that," she countered. "She could have. That's the point, right? And she said something about being responsible for people getting sick on some tonic she'd brewed up. They may have even died. She'll never pass the Virtues' spiritual fitness test." She hadn't been sure when she started to explain, but the more she talked, the more confident she became that it would work. That perhaps it might even be true.

Abraxas shifted away from her, and she immediately missed the heat of his touch, but she did not pull him back. "You want Lilitha to take the blame for Daniel's murder?"

"It's perfect, isn't it?"

131

"She would never confess."

"She will. Because we will make her."

His face clouded over.

She said, "Do you remember the first time you came to the Eden? You brought your lovers."

"Thralls. Whom I gave up for you, by the way," he said, giving her a long look.

"Can't you do the same to Lilitha?"

"They gave themselves to me in exchange for something they desired."

"I know what Lilitha desires," she said, thinking of how the girl had wanted so badly for Celeste to notice her, to think of her as her equal. "So all you need do is make the bargain, and she will be your thrall."

Abraxas shifted, uneasy. "Even if I do this, it will only gentle her. I cannot compel her to confess."

"I will wear the gloria."

Horror flashed across his face, so quickly she wasn't sure she had seen it at all, before his expression became unreadable. But his eyes lingered on the locket she still wore around her neck.

"You tame her will," she whispered, intense, "and I will make sure every Virtue in that room believes she is Daniel's murderer."

Abraxas's gaze was hooded. "You said that Tabor implied that Daniel had impregnated a Fallen girl, and she had come asking him for money."

"That's right."

"Celeste, that was Mariel."

Her mouth tightened, and her gaze flickered in annoyance. "And so you think she should be executed?" she asked, voice rising. "If that is true and this Daniel used her and threw her over, then he's the villain, is he not?" She was angry now. She had come up with the perfect solution, and he was telling her it was no good, implying that she was no good for thinking of it. "I know you don't like Mariel, but I didn't realize you'd be happy to see her dead."

"That is untrue."

"Is it? You've always hated her."

"I have never hated her. I've hated the way you use her as a shield."

"I don't know what you're talking about." She bristled.

"This, what we did tonight, this could be us every night for eternity. But you refuse because Mariel might need you."

The same argument they had had a hundred times. She thought that sleeping with him, again, would change things, but still he demanded too much. "I am not giving up my family for you."

"I can be your family. Do you not understand that? Why won't you let me in?"

"Because if I leave you, you will be fine. But if I leave Mariel, what will she have?"

His face was incredulous. "You think I am fine?" He gestured around his cabin, so far from his luxurious manse. "Does it look like I am fine?"

She could see that she had caused him pain, and that was something she would have to atone for one day, but now was not the time. "She needs me," she said simply.

"The way she needed Daniel?" he scoffed.

"What does that mean?"

"She killed him, Celeste!" he yelled, his frustration finally breaking into fury. "She killed him! In a lover's quarrel, a fit of rage, who knows? But if she was begging funds from Tabor for their unborn child, their relationship had already soured.

And now you want me to enthrall an innocent woman as her scapegoat? And you are willing to offer her up to die under Azrael's sword to save your murderous sister?"

She stared, shocked, until her temper exploded. She struck his cheek hard enough that the sound of it filled the room. And then she was striding across the room, pulling on her shift, her chemise, the sheath with the dagger, and then her blouse. Finally, her skirt and her coat. It wasn't quite proper, but it would do, and she had to get away from there. Get away from him.

Her shoes. Where were her shoes?

"Celeste."

He was beside her, still naked, still beautiful, and she hated him for it. She raised her hand to strike him again, but he caught her wrist, and then her dagger was in her free hand and at his neck.

"You are a demon," she hissed. "You do not get to judge me, you goddamned monster!"

His lip curled, part laugh and part sneer. "Damned? Yes, I do not deny it. But to say I am a monster when you stand before me asking me for what you are asking me? I am not the monster, Celeste."

She screamed in frustration and threw the dagger across the room. If he would not let her go, then she needed him to leave.

"Get out!" she shouted, shame and desperation making her irrational. "If I mean that little to you, get out!"

He flinched. "I did not say—"

"You speak of eternal love, of being my family, but when I need you most, you balk."

Abraxas drew himself up, wrapping himself in his pride. "I would have done anything for you. Do you not know that? And this is the thing you ask."

Celeste knew in that moment that Abraxas was right about one thing. She was the monster. Not because she was half-Fallen but because she was selfish and craven. He had accused her of using Mariel as a shield, as an excuse not to pursue the life she deserved, as a reason not to be with him. And he was right about all of it.

But what did being right matter when she could not change who she was? That was what she had told him when defending Mariel's innocence in killing the bird. Now she said the same to explain her own guilt.

"People don't change," she said thickly. "Not the fundamental part of them. This is who I am, Abraxas. Fallen and Elect all at once. Blessed and damned. I may love you, but I love Mariel more, and if you make me choose, I will pick her every time. Now, if you will not help, then let me go!"

She turned her back to him.

He was silent so long she thought he had left in some demonic way, but finally, she heard him moving around, gathering his clothes. His footsteps crossed the wooden floor, and he paused, the door open.

"I could never let you go, Celeste."

Oh, how his voice ached. But Mariel—she had to think of Mariel. If she did not give Lilitha to the Virtues, then Mariel would die. She hardened her heart, even though it cost her everything. Perhaps even her soul.

"God is cruel, Abraxas. You know that better than most."

She felt his gaze upon her back, but she could not turn to face him, could not let him see the tears that filled her eyes, the look of her own doubt upon her face.

"*Deus crudelis*," he whispered. "*Homo crudelior*."

She turned, a cry of anguish upon her lips.

But he was already gone.

CHAPTER 15

SHERIFF YBARRA CAME a few hours after dawn with two Virtues to take Lilitha away.

An hour after Abraxas had left, Celeste had heard a loud thump at the door. She had opened it to find the girl bound, gagged, and insensate, sagging against the wall. Abraxas was nowhere to be seen. She had dragged her inside and then gone down to the town to find the sheriff. She'd told him the story she had concocted, and he'd said he would rouse the Virtues necessary and meet her at the cabin.

She had sat in a chair, the same chair Abraxas had sat in to read his book as he waited for her to wake up. She tried not to think about him, about what they had done in that bed only hours ago and what she had said afterward to destroy it all. She would not let emotions sway her. She knew her purpose and what had to be done.

"You said she confessed it all?" Ybarra asked as they loaded Lilitha into a wagon.

"Do you know what a gloria is, Sheriff?" Celeste asked.

His brow furrowed in confusion. "I'm afraid not."

The Virtue who had come to aid in Lilitha's arrest, an Order

137

of Michael, slammed the wagon door shut. Ybarra jumped, but Celeste only smiled.

"I imagine a gloria has something to do with the Virtues," Ybarra said, "but beyond that, I cannot say." He sounded uneasy. "I am not sure that I want to know."

"Would that I could have stayed ignorant of such a thing myself," she admitted, "although I see the usefulness of its purpose now. Trust that it will reveal the truth."

He nodded, more in sympathy than in agreement, and took to his mount. The Virtue driving the wagon spurred the pulling horse forward, and the wagon surged ahead on rattling wheels. Ybarra paused. "Would you like a ride back to town?"

"No, I'd rather walk."

He looked doubtful.

"I need to make a stop before I come to court."

"Have it your way." He tipped his hat and turned his mare, and then he and the wagon retreated down the path back to town.

She did not follow but instead took a detour down a small trail off the main road. The way had once been as familiar as the contours of her own face, but now it was overgrown. She trod carefully through the low brush lest her feet tangle in the vines. Presently, she arrived at her destination.

The fence was still there, the same one where she'd buried the baby bird. The house itself was empty, a sign on the gate declaring it had been sold to the Tabor Land Corporation. Someone must have lived here recently, but now they had moved on. She entered the yard, her heart racing, as if something dreadful waited within. But there was nothing here to harm her but memories, and while they had their ways, she had done enough harm to herself these past few hours that a memory could do no worse.

She sat on the porch steps and closed her eyes. She could feel the ghosts of her childhood home stir around her. Could almost hear the voices of her mother and the occasional laugh of her father when he'd come to call on her and she and Mariel had been made to sleep out under the eaves.

Again, that day played out in her head, and for the thousandth time, she hated herself for going with her father, for leaving her sister behind. And for the thousandth time, she swore that she would never do it again, no matter the cost.

Mariel's spirit seemed to hover near, watchful. So real Celeste could almost reach out and touch her. "I won't fail you again," she whispered to that memory. "I swear it on my soul."

She expected thunder to roll at such a vow, but there was only the rising sun warm against her face and the call of birdsong welcoming the day. She sat for a while longer, wishing for all the world that Abraxas was there and that she might confide in him, but she knew he would never hold her again, never argue theology with her, never kiss her neck.

Now he was just another memory, as out of reach as all her other ghosts.

JUST AS IT had been on her first visit, the territorial courthouse was packed. Not only with lawmen and reporters but with many of the citizens of Goetia, Elect and Fallen alike. The Virtues may have silenced the *Howler*, but word had spread anyway, and now all of Goetia knew that Mariel's trial was to take place today.

Most of the townsfolk were gathered on the courthouse steps, ready to witness the aftermath of justice served or, if necessary, protest its violation. She thought she saw Hypatia and Zeke in the crowd, and she ducked her head, blending in before they could spot her. She could not face her friends with the blood that stained her hands. She had stolen Zeke's trike, his most prized possession, the thing he'd poured his heart and soul into, and abandoned it on the mountain. She had not even thought of retrieving it until just now. And there were no words for what she had done to Hypatia. She wondered if Hypatia even knew what had happened to Lilitha or if she thought her love had just run off. And what would she think when she found out the woman she loved was a murderer? Would she believe it? Would it break her heart?

Celeste looked up to find the statue of the archangel Michael looming above her, and she shuddered.

This time, the deputy guarding the door did stop her, and she explained in a low voice who she was and why she was there. His eyes widened, but he let her through with little fuss. She was, after all, expected.

Inside, the chaos lessened. Here were mostly Virtues in their white robes and porcelain masks and, cordoned off to the side, the laypeople—reporters and law clerks—who would be waiting to hear the verdict and relay it to the people outside. She looked for Grace Walter, holding out some foolish hope that the reporter would be there in her smart suit waiting to get the scuttlebutt, but she was not. Celeste did see Mrs. Alameda in her funeral black, a handkerchief clutched in her gloved hands.

An Order of Michael pointed her toward the elevator at the far end of the lobby, where a Virtue, indistinguishable from any other, motioned her to join him. It could only be Ibrahim. He excused himself from his compatriots and came to greet her.

"Miss Semyaza."

"Virtue Ibrahim."

"I received some interesting news from Sheriff Ybarra earlier," he said, voice pitched low for privacy. "It seems congratulations are in order."

"There is still a murder and still a Fallen woman facing a death sentence," she said. "I would think you would be more circumspect."

"I only meant you have successfully brought forth another credible suspect, which can only bode well for your sister's fate. The court will have the ultimate say, of course, but I cannot imagine your questioning will not be persuasive."

"There is something else you need to know." She told him of her encounter with Tabor and the man's demise.

She could not see his expression, but she was sure he was smiling. "We are already aware of it. I dare to say his death eases several problems the Orders were having with his outlaw behavior. We all agree his passing was God's will."

Celeste stared, disbelieving. "A demon lord took his head with a hellfire sword."

He lifted his gaze toward heaven. "The Almighty works in mysterious ways. And now that the mine will be under new ownership, I expect divinity production to reach a record high. An exciting time for Goetia."

She stared at the man. She knew he was dishonest, but she still found herself in shock. "The new owner wouldn't happen to be you, would it, Mr. Ibrahim?"

"Why, Miss Semyaza, what a clever mind you have."

"Did you set Mariel up from the beginning?"

"You will not believe me, but no. We had nothing to do with Daniel's murder, as your Lilitha will no doubt testify. But his death did afford us an opportunity, and heaven bless you, Miss Semyaza, you rose to the occasion and allowed that opportunity to flourish into good fortune, indeed."

"You used me."

"Of course."

"He tried to kill me."

"But he did not succeed." He leaned in. "I do apologize for that, but all's well that ends well, yes?" Above them, a bell tolled the hour. "It is almost time. Why don't you go talk to Mariel and prepare her for the good news? I'll see you within the chamber at the hour."

"There's one other thing," Celeste said quickly. "A mechanical trike. I left it at Tabor's laboratory."

"I will inquire as to its fate. Is there anything else?"

"No. Thank you."

Ibrahim waved a waiting Virtue over, an anonymous face behind a white mask marked with Chamuel's scales of justice. "Take the *advocatus* to see the accused. Oh, and my pin?"

Celeste made a show of checking her pockets. "I don't have it," she lied. "I must have lost it at Tabor's lab."

Irritation flashed across his face. "Perhaps it will show up. If you do find it, I expect you will return it."

"Of course," she acceded.

"If you'll excuse me." And then he was gone.

She wasn't sure why she kept his pin. It was petty, but if she could cause him even the smallest inconvenience, she wished to do it. Besides, it might be useful in the future.

She followed the Virtue to the now familiar elevator. This time, the elevator stopped only a floor below the main level and opened onto a plain but well-lit hallway. He led her down a row of cells, half of them populated by men who looked like the kind of common criminal one found on any given night along Perdition. They shouted and rattled the bars as they passed, but Celeste kept her gaze forward.

They reached the end of the hall and passed through a door

to another cluster of cells, and there, alone on a plain bench, was Mariel. She looked much improved from before, bathed and groomed, and a plain calico day dress had replaced her bloody Aventum finery. It was two sizes too large, but Mariel had tied it in a way that made it look like a royal gown and herself a princess in it.

"Celeste!" she cried, and rushed forward.

Someone had placed a wooden chair in front of the cell bars, and Celeste sat.

"I will return to collect you once the trial is ready to begin," the Virtue said, and then he was gone, and Celeste was alone with her sister.

"Oh, Celeste," Mariel gushed, "I don't know what you did, but they've been treating me like royalty since last you came! They don't want to, I can tell that much, and they still curse me under their breath, no doubt. But I've had a bath, and I'm wearing a clean dress, although I'm sure it's a hand-me-down. Did I mention they fed me a proper meal? And tea. They even offered me a dime novel, but you know I don't read. And..." She trailed off. "What's wrong? Why aren't you speaking?"

Celeste studied her sister, looking for the woman she had failed to see before. The Mariel in front of her was the one she thought she knew. Kind, beautiful, and admirably innocent despite life's tragedies. But this Mariel was a lie, a facade her sister wore for Celeste's benefit. How could she not have seen it? *Because when it comes to Mariel, you only see what you want to see*, Abraxas whispered, and Celeste clenched her jaw, allowing all her anger at Mariel's deception to rise to the surface.

"Celeste. What's wrong?"

"You can stop pretending, Mariel," she said, voice sharp. "I know the truth."

Mariel went still. "I don't know what you heard, but—"

"I know about Daniel!" she shouted. She took a deep breath and made herself lower her voice, although there was no one to hear them. "I know you were seeing him behind my back. I know about his wife and his business partner you tried to blackmail." Celeste stared her sister down. "And I know you took a butchering knife from the kitchen at the Eden and killed him. The only thing I don't know is why. And why you didn't trust me enough to tell me."

Mariel trembled, a hand over her mouth, and for a moment Celeste thought perhaps she had gotten it wrong. But then her sister lowered her hand and clapped. Once, twice, three times, slowly.

"Well, goddamn, Celeste. I didn't know you had it in you."

She frowned. "What does that mean?"

"It means," Mariel said, leaning back on her bench, "that I thought for sure I was going to have to keep playing the innocent my whole damn life, just to keep you off my back."

Celeste flinched. "I never asked you to pretend."

"No?" Her voice rose an octave in mimicry. "Mariel, don't drink laudanum. Mariel, it's not safe to walk home alone. Mariel, don't step out with a man." Her tone turned cruel. "While you're out there pirooting with a goddamned demon."

Celeste stared, at a loss for words. "I was only trying to protect you," she finally said.

"Well, who asked you to?"

That stung. "But Dad left you..."

"And good riddance. Isn't that always what you say, Celeste? That he was an awful man, so why would I have wanted to go with him?" She drew a cigarillo from the pocket of her dress and lit it. "If you ask me, I dodged a bullet, because he sure did a number on you."

"Ah, that's not fair," Celeste murmured. "Mama did her share, too."

Mariel laughed at that, loud and brash. "Well, at least that's the truth. Neither of them was worth the skin they wore."

"Since when do you smoke?" Celeste asked absently. "Never mind, give me one." She leaned in, and Mariel handed her a thin cigarette, struck a match, and lit it. The smoke immediately soothed her nerves. "How did you get these?"

"One of the Virtues. We traded."

"With what? No, I don't what to know that, either." She exhaled, hands rubbing along her thighs, trying to think, but her mind was still reeling. She looked up. "Have I been that awful?" she asked.

"Yes." Mariel sighed. "No. But heaven and hell, Celeste, you've got to let me breathe."

"Was this my fault?"

"Daniel? Heavens, no." She sat up. "Oh, he was a sly one, and I should have known it, but he was charming and a real belvidere, you know? Eyes like the spring skies and so smooth-tongued. But trust a man who knows his value to deny a woman hers."

"What happened?"

Mariel took a deep drag. "We were going to run away together. I mean, that's what he said. Go somewhere where they wouldn't even know I was Fallen, wouldn't recognize the Mark for what it was. He promised." She waved her hand, brushing the smoke away. "I know what you're going to say. I sound like a lovestruck fool. But I wanted it, Celeste. I wanted it!" She slammed her hand against the bench. "Not just him but everything he could give me. A new life in a new place, performing on a big stage, not just the same old thing at the Eden every night. But then I found out I was pregnant. At first, he was supportive, saying it was all daisies, but then he stopped coming around so often. Well, I wasn't going to be tossed aside, so I did a little asking around."

"His wife," Celeste said. "And Tabor, his business partner."

"That's right," Mariel said. "I didn't rat him out, just did some inquiring."

"They knew what you were about."

Mariel shrugged. "Bully for them. If he was going to ruin me, well, two could play at that game. But then he showed up in some devilish costume on Aventum, so I snuck him into the back, no one the wiser, Hypatia too busy holding court to notice. I thought maybe he'd come around, and things would be all right after all. And at first, it looked like I was right. He was passionate and demanding, like always. But after, we're lying there, my skirts barely straight, and he tells me it's over. Tells me I shouldn't have gone running my mouth like I had, and he's a doctor, so here's an abortive"—her honey-ringed eyes flared bright with hate—"and I should take it. Told me that once the baby was gone, I shouldn't bother him anymore and that he never wanted to see me again!" She pressed a hand to her belly. She had not started to show yet, but Celeste had no doubt she carried Daniel's child.

"So you killed him?"

She lifted her chin. "That was just the side effect. I took his manhood."

"Saints and sinners, Mariel."

"I don't regret it." Her bright eyes were hard. "Let them kill me for it, those hypocrites. I'll curse them all the way down to hell."

Celeste ran her hands over her face. "They're not going to kill you."

"What do you mean?"

"I've found someone else to pin the murder on."

Mariel frowned. "Who?"

"Lilitha."

Her eyes widened in surprise. "Hypatia's girl?"

Celeste nodded.

Mariel shifted, uneasy. "I don't know, Celeste. I never had anything against Lilitha. And Hypatia sure is sweet on her."

"I said that I'd protect you," Celeste said fiercely. "This is what it takes."

"But how? She'll deny it."

"Abraxas has compelled her."

"Abraxas?" Now she looked doubly shocked. "You went to him?"

"Only to help you, to save you."

Mariel whistled low. "And what did your demon lord say to all this?"

"This was his farewell gift." She roughly wiped at the tears she could not keep from gathering. "So he's not my demon lord anymore."

"I'm sorry, Cece." And it sounded like she meant it.

Celeste moved closer to the bars. "Listen, Mariel. You cannot tell anyone what you've told me. Right now, they think Lilitha is the killer, and you are innocent, and… and it will stay that way."

"Are you sure?" She sounded so young. She might play the tough, but Celeste could see she had not been completely wrong about her sister. There was an innocence there, no matter her deeds to the contrary.

"We're sisters. If I must choose, then I choose you. I choose family."

"Sisters," Mariel echoed, but she didn't sound as sure, her eyes lingering on Celeste as if this time she was the one who had failed to see her real sister until this very minute.

Footsteps sounded in the hall, the door opened, and the Virtue was back.

"The Circle is ready for you."

Mariel stood, stubbing out her cigarillo. The Virtue unlocked her cell, restrained her hands in irons, and marched her forward, Celeste trailing behind.

CHAPTER 16

THE CIRCLE'S COURT chamber was at the top of the building, down the hall from Ibrahim's office in the opposite direction from the elevator. Celeste and Mariel stood waiting in a small atrium. From the window, Celeste could see all of Goetia and, above it, the mountain of Abaddon, its smaller peaks the Hands and the highest, always capped in snow, the peak called Abaddon's Heart.

Once, after a late night at the faro table, Celeste had asked Abraxas to tell her what happened the day Abaddon fell, and he had looked at her so long she thought she had offended him. Finally, he'd said, "*Domine miserere damnati.*"

"Lord have mercy on the damned," she'd translated, pleased to show off the Latin she had been learning.

"Have you ever seen an angel, Celeste?" he'd asked, voice wistful. "They are not like you and me. They are fire and wings and eyes and beauty so bright you cannot look upon it. Such was Abaddon, one of the best of Lucifer's brethren. We called him Doom and Destroyer, and he came to the battlefield with an army of locusts at his back, plague in his every breath. It was Abaddon who led the charge that day against cruel Azrael,

149

the Angel of Death himself, and for a while, our victory seemed sure. But something changed. A shift in the wind, a moment of distraction. Who can say? Abaddon fell, Azrael's sword through his heart. And lo, we demons wept.

"We fought on, of course, with our hellfire and black blades, but without our leader…" He'd lifted his shoulder in a shrug. "The battle ended in our surrender, for what is heaven if not merciful?" His voice had been thick with bitterness. "Both sides agreed that someone had to stay to watch over Abaddon's body, and I loved him so well that I volunteered."

She had not expected that. "You chose to stay?"

"I was loyal and could not fathom leaving him behind."

"And you are still here?"

He'd drunk from the glass of bourbon at his side. "Ever vigilant."

She had not meant to ask, but she had to know. "Do you wish to return to hell someday?"

His crimson eyes had dimmed. "What is hell to me now but a memory? Who can say if I am even welcome after all this time?"

"It doesn't matter," she had assured him. "Goetia is your home now, and you have me."

He had looked at her, long and contemplative, and said, "I have you, Celeste."

She had not understood then what she knew now, that in that moment, he had made a choice. And she had repaid his loyalty with cruelty.

"Celeste?"

Now she shook herself from her reverie and turned back to a waiting Mariel.

"Are you okay?"

She smoothed a hand across her skirts and took a deep breath. "I'm fine."

Mariel smiled, but she looked nervous.

"Do you remember that baby bird you caught when we were small?" Celeste asked, thinking to distract her.

"What?"

"That bird. You petted it, and its feathers came off. And you were so distraught that you sobbed and sobbed, and I had to give you warm milk and put you to bed to calm you down."

Mariel's mouth turned down. "You thought I was crying about a bird?"

"Weren't you?"

Mariel laughed, a harsh sound. "I plucked those feathers off, thinking to give them to you, like a present. But you gave me this look, like I was a monster. That's what spooked me. I didn't care a fig about that bird." She shook her head. "I cared about you. What you thought of me."

Celeste stared, stunned.

"It died, you know," Mariel said. "I'd crushed it, not on purpose, but I went back to bury it, worried that you'd see it, but a hawk or something must have gotten it, 'cause I never did find the body. Just a bit of blood and feathers."

"Are you ready?" A Virtue stood holding the door to the trial chamber open.

Mariel nodded. "Let's go."

He released her shackles and led them in.

The chamber was not large, but it was filled to capacity, and for an instant, the heat of so many bodies knocked Celeste back a step. The room was shaped in a semicircle. Directly before her was a judge upon a dais, and facing him were two tables with accompanying chairs. Everywhere else were Virtues, so many that the room seemed filled with phantoms. Above the main chamber ran a balcony where a handful of Elect citizens, who had a stake in the proceedings or were otherwise invited to attend, sat. The only one she recognized was Mrs. Alameda. The woman sensed Celeste's gaze and began to turn toward her, but Celeste quickly looked away.

Beside her, Mariel made a sound of dismay. Her hand found Celeste's, and she held on tight. They walked to the empty table, hand in hand.

Across from them was the *accusator*. He was a tall man in a black waistcoat and jacket, his dark hair oiled and curling around his ears. He glanced briefly at Celeste and then dismissed her with a contemptuous sniff.

Once they were seated, the judge called the trial to order.

"I understand there has been an unexpected development," he began, his voice carrying effortlessly through the room. Celeste noticed he spoke into a mechanical amplifier. "Another suspect has been discovered by the *advocatus*." He gestured, and from a door in the side of the room, two Virtues brought forth Lilitha.

She dragged between them, limp and almost lifeless, and they pressed her into a chair in the middle of the room. Her eyes roamed the room as if looking for something, and Celeste realized she must be searching for Abraxas. It was disquieting, and Celeste found herself looking away.

She glanced over at Mariel. Her sister was silent, but her eyes were huge and fixed on Lilitha.

"Bring forth the gloria," the judge ordered.

The Virtue acting as a bailiff brought a small velvet-covered box over and set it before Celeste. Ibrahim had warned her that she would be required to wear one at the trial, and she was ready. It was meant to compel its wearer to speak the truth, or at least what they believed to be the truth, and uttering a lie would sear the tongue, burning it to ash within the speaker's mouth.

She touched her hand to the hidden pendant Abraxas had given her before she had first come to the courthouse, the one that allowed her to deny the edict of the gloria. He had not asked for it back, even knowing what she planned to do.

She opened the box and took the golden mechanical cicada in hand. It vibrated against her palm.

"What is it?" Mariel whispered, sounding horrified.

"An invention of the Virtues. It forces you to tell the truth."

"And you mean to wear it?"

"I must."

"And if you lie?"

A trickle of fear shivered down her back. "It will maim me."

"Celeste…"

She should have explained Abraxas's pendant, but there had not been time before, and now it was too late. "I have a plan."

"I cannot let you do it."

"It's too late," she whispered, glancing over at the *accusator*, who was staring reproachfully at them. "Just trust me."

Mariel shook her head, slowly and then more fiercely. "This is all wrong," she murmured. "I cannot let this happen. To you, to Lilitha. When it was my doing."

"Quiet, Mariel."

"Damn you, Celeste," she hissed. "Stop telling me what to do!" She lifted her chin, as proud and defiant as any fallen angel. "If I am bound for hell, I will not drag you down with me. And I will go on my own terms."

She lunged for the gloria, catching Celeste by surprise. She snatched the metal cicada from her palm, and before Celeste could stop her, Mariel had stuck it into her mouth.

Celeste watched in horror as Mariel gagged, mouth wide. The bug's legs wrapped around her tongue, and its wings began to flutter. Mariel swayed on her feet, then staggered to the center of the room.

The crowd erupted into shouts and confusion.

The judge hammered his gavel, yelling, "A witness cannot be compelled! A witness cannot be compelled!"

"Mariel!" Celeste rushed forward, but the *accusator* seized her and held her back. "Mariel, no!" But her pleas were lost in the burgeoning chaos.

"It was my hand!" Mariel cried.

The judge froze, his arm still raised. The Virtues, shouting and pointing, stilled. Only Lilitha moved. She lifted her head, gaze fixed upon Mariel.

"I killed Daniel Alameda." Mariel looked around the room, her golden-rimmed eyes ablaze. "It was my hand that held the knife and ruined his life. The same way he ruined mine."

Shouting erupted again, this time in rage.

"She is with child!" Celeste shouted. It was the only thing she could think that might slow their vengeance. "She carries Virtue Daniel's child!"

The crowd fell into shocked silence.

Celeste threw the *accusator* off and went to Mariel, who was weeping and grotesque, with the gloria still in her mouth. Celeste reached for it, and at her touch, its wings ceased to flutter, and its legs contracted. Once it was in hand, she hurled it away.

Mariel collapsed into her arms. "I couldn't let you do it," she whispered. "You're my sister."

"I know," Celeste soothed, even though her heart shattered. "It will be okay."

She dropped them gently to the floor, Mariel cradled in her arms. She raised her head and spoke to the Circle. "If you sentence her to death, you sentence an innocent child to die, too!"

"She murdered its father!" The *accusator* spoke for the first time. "And confessed to the crime, not compelled, but by her own volition. What life would it have, burdened by such sin?"

"I will take the child!"

The voice came from above in the balcony, and all eyes turned upward. It was Daniel's widow, Mrs. Alameda, who had spoken.

"I'll take the child and the mother. I will raise the child as my own, and…" She hesitated. "I would seek to rehabilitate the mother. If the Circle will allow it."

Murmurs rippled through the crowd until the judge ordered everyone to be silent.

"You would take the murderess of your husband into your home?" he asked, incredulous.

"Yes. The fate of a woman deceived by a man is a sorry thing." She glanced toward Mariel. "I believe we have that in common. I see that now. Plus, I am alone, and I think I could help."

Celeste thought to protest, but what could she do? Mrs. Alameda had been cruel to her, thinking she was one of Daniel's girls, but that did not mean she would mistreat his child. And while she would save Mariel from the woman's tender care if she could, she had just stayed her execution, and her sympathy seemed genuine. Surely a life in the house on Gethsemane was better than no life at all.

Celeste turned to the judge as he delivered his verdict.

"I commend Mariel Semyaza into Ann Alameda's care for the term of her pregnancy. Once the child is born, Mariel Semyaza will appear before the Circle again. If she has been rehabilitated, she will be spared, but if she has failed to show remorse for her actions, she will face the justice she has earned, and her soul shall be delivered to hell. Until that time in the future, no member of this body of Virtues shall interfere. Gentlemen Elect, we are adjourned."

He slammed the gavel down.

Celeste shivered and pulled her sister close. Mariel had still not made a sound, but she could feel her shoulders shudder, from grief or relief, she was not sure.

"I won't leave you, Mariel," she said. "I promise."

Now Mariel raised her head. Her cheeks were dry, and she calmly disentangled herself from her sister's arms. "It's time you let me go, Celeste," she said. "This next part I need to do on my own."

"I'll visit you."

"I'd prefer you didn't. At least for a while."

Celeste felt a strange sensation in her chest, as if some burden had been lifted from her heart, followed immediately by a dizzying feeling of loss.

"Are you sure?" she asked.

"I'll be okay," Mariel said. She pushed herself to her feet and started toward the bailiff. He stood waiting, Mrs. Alameda by his side. "And Celeste..."

She looked up.

"I know it's not much, but thank you. And tell Abraxas I thank him, too. And... I'm sorry. For everything."

And then she was gone, and Celeste was left kneeling alone on the floor.

CHAPTER 17

IT HAD BEGUN to rain. At first, only enough to wet the ash that clogged the streets, but by the time Celeste had passed the boardinghouse on Elysium, rain was filling the gutters and dripping from the eaves. She wondered who had claimed her old room and when she might be able to retrieve the belongings she had left behind and send Mariel's things to the house on Gethsemane. But that was a problem for another day.

She walked past the offices of the *Howler* and could not help but look for Grace in the window, but there was only Mr. Song at the typesetter. She turned before she reached the Excelsior Hotel and the neighborhood of mansions just beyond. The rain had soaked through her coat and boots.

By the time she reached Perdition Street, it had turned into a downpour, and the rain fell in great sweeping sheets. It was still early, even though the sun was lost somewhere behind the low clouds and gray gloom, and only a few determined merrymakers populated the various pleasure houses and saloons. The Eden had reopened, and its doors were flung wide despite the storm. There was a poster board over the cracked window advertising a new songstress, someone come down from the capital. Celeste could not read her name through the deluge.

The heavy rains had washed out the bridge to the Drench, so she took the steep and mud-slicked path down through the ravine. She slipped more than once, but she finally made it, skirts torn and hands bruised from catching herself against the rocks. To her left was the way to Abraxas's cabin. She took the road to her right.

She passed through the gate, past the Tabor Land Corporation sign, and up to the porch. She hadn't thought to try the door when she was there before, but she did now. It opened into a house she had once called her home—and would again, if she could convince Ibrahim to sell it back to her. She wasn't sure where she would get the funds for it, but she had some talents and a bit of savings. She would find a way.

The first thing she did was open the window. The rain blew in, hard spittle against her face. It would soak the floorboards soon enough, maybe even settle to rot if she didn't replace them.

The people before her had left their furniture. It was old and shabby, and when Celeste sat on the narrow bed, it sagged in protest. Resigned, she curled up on the worn mattress, wet and filthy and lost, and closed her eyes.

The night settled in. At first, she did not sleep, even though she was exhausted. Finally, she drifted off, only to awake in darkness, aware of a presence behind her.

Soft cotton fell across her body, and she smelled rosewood and amber.

She did not turn or lift her head, afraid to face him or, worse, to find he wasn't truly there at all.

"I have lingered too long in Goetia," he said, his voice a whisper. "It has changed me in ways I do not recognize."

"Abraxas..." she began.

"Please, Celeste. Let me speak. We are not so different, you and I. I blamed you for clinging to Mariel, but I think I am guilty of the same. I have stayed here for eons, watching over a corpse."

"Mariel left me," she blurted, unable to hold the grief of it back.

"Ahh..."

She turned to face him. He was only a shadow in the dark room, less than a sliver of the moonless night.

"That means we can be together," she said, sounding more eager, more fervent, than she meant to. "There's nothing to come between us now, Abraxas. I am yours, body and soul."

The rain beat against the roof, steady as a heartbeat.

"Sometimes we cling too tightly to people whom we should let go," he said.

Her heart sped up, and she dared to hope. She rose to her feet and moved toward him, her arms outstretched.

He stepped back. "I am speaking about myself."

She let her arms drop, her face hot with shame. "I know that I have done the unforgivable," she whispered. "And yet I ask your forgiveness."

"Demonkind do not forgive, Celeste." White teeth flashed in the darkness. "You should know better than that."

"I will make amends," she offered, words tumbling from her tongue in desperation. "To you, Hypatia and Zeke, Lilitha, too."

"Lilitha is mine," he said, voice dark. "She bargained. It is out of your hands now."

"I will take her place."

His look was reproachful. "Trade? When I already have you both, should I wish it? I don't think so."

"Abraxas?" She did not recognize him like this. Cruel and unbending.

She heard the scuff of his feet against the floorboards as he paced away. "The problem, Celeste, is that what you're offering? I don't want it anymore."

She flinched at his viciousness, but she would not beg.

"Then what do you want?" she asked, chin raised.

"I am leaving."

What was left of her heart buckled in despair, but she swallowed the pain. "Where will you go?"

"Hell, if it will have me. But if not..." He shrugged. "The world is a wide place."

"Then one day, I will see you in hell, Abraxas," she said, as challenge and threat and vow.

Thunder rolled, somewhere nearby.

He touched a long-nailed finger to his brow and inclined his head. She caught the edge of a satisfied smile.

"I await the day, Celeste."

And then he was gone.

AFTER A WHILE, she walked to the bed, took the blanket Abraxas had given her, and wrapped it around her shoulders. She went to sit on the edge of the porch.

Dawn must be near, but she could not see it through the downpour, still falling steady and relentless. She lifted her face to the sky, but even the rain that fell from heaven could not quite wash her clean.

ACKNOWLEDGMENTS

Most people don't know this, but I was a pretty religious kid. And while I am not religious now, the mythology and vocabulary of Judeo-Christianity is imbedded deep in my bones. I went to Catholic schools for the first eight years of my education where people like my 8th grade religion teacher, Mr. Shields, instilled a lifelong curiosity about religion. Later, I attended Yale as an undergrad and majored in Religious Studies and there had some amazing teachers as well, most of them long retired but never forgotten. And, after, I received a Master's in Theology from Union Theological, where I was honored to work with many minds on the forefront of radical reimaginings of Black and feminist religious praxis.

None of that great academic stuff made it into this book, although I do owe a debt of gratitude (and perhaps an apology) to all my wonderful religion teachers throughout my formal education.

What did make it into this book was a trip to Silverton, Colorado, some deep thoughts about the trope of the "tragic mulatto" and the need to upend that, an interest in the lives of the people who lived on the margins of the Old West, ten years as a practicing attorney, and a story sparked to live in equal measure from Guillermo del Toro's remake of *Nightmare Alley*, P. Djèlí Clark's *A Master of Djinn*, and a handful of Urban Fantasy novels about angels and demons.

Thanks to my editor, Joe Monti, for letting me write this quirky little novella and allowing me to bring all my disparate interests together. Being creative in the midst of the COVID-

19 pandemic was a challenge, as was getting out of bed and continuing to function. You gave me the freedom to explore something outside of what I might normally write, and that is very appreciated.

Thanks to my agent, Sara Megibow, who continues to be both friend and business partner.

Thanks to Turquoise Apocalypse—Lauren C. Teffeau, Sarena Ulibarri, Brian Hinson, and Ian Tregillis. Special shoutout to Ian, who also has Judeo-Christian mythos deep in his bones and whose enthusiasm for the story kept me going.

Thanks to my husband, Michael Roanhorse, who could never remember what the story was about—is this the one with Serapio?—but who nonetheless cheered me on, fed me, caffeinated me, and is the best partner I could ask for.

Thanks to my daughter, Maya, who did remember what the story was about and advised me on plot issues accordingly. As always, you are a bright light in my life.

Thanks to the team at Gallery Books/Saga Press for all the work and dedication and love. This book wouldn't exist without you.

FIND US ONLINE!

www.rebellionpublishing.com

/rebellionpub   /rebellionpublishing   /rebellionpublishing

SIGN UP TO OUR NEWSLETTER!

rebellionpublishing.com/newsletter

YOUR REVIEWS MATTER!

Enjoy this book? Got something to say?

Leave a review on Amazon, GoodReads or with your
favourite bookseller and let the world know!